WEREWOLF'S PRINCESS

Big City Lycans
Book Five

New York Times and USA Today Bestselling Author

Eve Langlais

Copyright Werewolf's Princess © Eve Langlais 2022/2023

Cover Art © by Melony Paradise of ParadiseCoverDesign.com 2022

Produced in Canada

Published by Eve Langlais

http://www.EveLanglais.com

eBook: ISBN: 978 1 77384 387 2

Print ISBN: 978 1 77384 388 9

PROLOGUE

MORE THAN A DECADE AGO...

LONDON'S WEATHER matched Brock's mood. Cold, wet, miserable, and gray.

Not usually one prone to melancholy, Brock hadn't been his usual cheerful self since the military discharged him. Actually, that whole disaffected feeling started in the prison where he got turned into a werewolf.

It wasn't as exciting as it sounded. For one, he couldn't tell anyone. He knew how that would end. Either with him in a cage being poked and forced to run in mazes or with a bullet to the head.

Neither sounded like any fun.

He'd been told by his creator—a man he and his

buddies had nicknamed Scarecrow on account he was a shell of himself—to A) tell no one, B) find a Pack to join, and C) don't knock up any chicks. He'd already mastered A. As for C, the first woman who winked at him when he got out of the military had him testing his equipment—with a condom, of course. To his relief, everything worked as expected, and as an added bonus, he saw an increase in stamina that the string of ladies after approved of.

Don't judge. He'd almost died. A man was allowed to comfort himself. As to those who would say he should have been leery, Scarecrow had said not to impregnate, implying sex was okay.

Back to B, the whole "join a Pack" thing. That hadn't gone so well.

Turned out it wasn't that hard to sniff out a local pack. The first thing Brock did in a new city was go exploring until his nose found a werewolf. Given they didn't seem to have as keen a sense of smell as Brock, he usually had to go up to them and introduce himself.

"Hey, can you help a brother out? I'm looking for a Pack to join."

That statement led to him being taken to the leader, whom they called Alpha.

Said leader took one look at Brock and was like, *"Not happening, buddy."* When asked why, they always said, *"Ain't room for two alphas in the pack."*

Didn't matter how many times Brock said he had no interest in leading a Pack, no one would take a chance on him.

He might have managed to beg a spot in Quinn's— one of two military brothers changed with him—new Pack, but given his troubles, he didn't want to fuck up his friend's shot at a normal-ish life. Hence why Brock left North America, not ready to give up. Eventually he'd find a place that felt like home.

He doubted it would be London. A few days here, wandering in the crowds, and he'd not picked up a single Lycan scent. Not one. It was almost unheard of. Surely a place as big and old as London had a Pack?

He noticed he'd picked up a shadow about two blocks from the clock tower. A good one, too, since he couldn't seem to catch a glimpse of them in any of the storefront windows. Probably a mugger. This time of night, a tourist-looking guy like him would make a ripe target.

He shoved his hands into his pockets and whistled. Might as well. The noise of London made it impossible to filter sound into anything worth identifying. The city never got fully quiet. He kind of liked it. The quiet was when his brain got too loud.

The mugger held off as Brock slid into an alley well before the clock tower situated on the corner of The Palace of Westminster. Restoration on the clock had

3

just finished, and it had been opened to the public again. The UK public. Only residents could visit during the day.

The crafty went at night.

Brock waited for the shadow to enter the alley and uttered an annoyed, "Can you hurry up? I've got an appointment to keep."

The person possessed a tall lanky grace, his pale skin appearing as if he never went out in the day. He had a slight beard on his square chin. Dressed in a suit, he didn't resemble any muggers Brock had ever encountered.

And he smelled—

A sensitive sniffer, Brock grimaced. "Jeezus, man, did you bathe in a vat of cologne? You know you're only supposed to dab."

"Stop talking." The voice tried to sound stern, and the eyes got an angry crinkle.

Brock sighed. "I thought London had some of the wiliest muggers in the world. You are really disappointing me."

"Would you shut up and put your hands out to the side?"

"Like this?" he asked, spreading them, looking like a welcoming victim.

"About time. I just wanted a snack before dealing

with—" The mumbling man neared, and Brock's hand shot out, grabbing him by the throat.

"I told you, I have an appointment to keep, so consider this a warning. Go back to mommy or daddy's house. Get online and find a real job. Maybe one that will teach you to be less useless because mugging is not your thing."

Wide eyes stared. The mouth gaped. The fellow didn't struggle, but he did whisper, "You're not supposed to be here."

"What's that supposed to mean?" Brock asked, trying not to sneeze at the strong perfume.

"I'm going to tell."

"A tattletale too? Can't say as I'm surprised." Brock lost the battle and sneezed. While he did his best to cover his mouth with the crook of his free arm, the mugger still whined.

"Ew. That's disgusting."

"Blame your eau de what da fuck. Take some advice and ditch the cologne." He thrust the mugger from him, who ogled him for only a second before running. Fast little fucker.

Brock went on his way, having studied maps beforehand so he knew where to go. The Palace holding Big Ben also doubled as the House of Commons, and it was through a utility door held open by a janitor— whom he'd bribed after discovering him online in a forum offering after-hour tours—that he entered and made his way from the Commons section to the clock tower.

To his surprise, the hairs on his nape lifted as he trod the empty halls, using the route recommended by the janitor, who knew where the cameras sat and which ones his buddy placed on a loop to facilitate their side trade. A glance over his shoulder showed no one shadowing, and yet he couldn't rid himself of the nagging sense he wasn't alone.

Wishful thinking? After all, Brock had felt isolated most of his life. His birth family, while well meaning, were highbrow scholars who didn't understand a guy like Brock who preferred to work with hands. He didn't mind getting dirty and dared to join the army, making his bum brother, the poet who lived in the basement, the better son. He'd not had contact with them in years. The military was his family once he left home. The men he served with became his true brothers. Alas, due to his captivity, he only had two brothers left: Quinn who'd joined a Pack in Canada, and Gunner, who was going through an existential crisis.

It took the keycard Brock borrowed, along with some actual keys, to get inside Big Ben and climb the three hundred some steps to the top. Once there, he marveled at the inner workings of the clock. Kind of cool.

As he was about to explore further, a soft but very feminine voice stopped him dead.

"You're trespassing." A glance showed a woman, her shapely figure wearing all black, which included a hood, sitting high up on a beam.

"As are you." He offered her a smile.

Her leap had his eyes widening as she barely bent her knees as she landed and strode for him, a sashaying curvy figure that literally took his breath. A glance within her deep cowl showed she wore a fabric mask that covered her from the nose down.

"I have every right to be here. You don't. Your kind are forbidden in London."

"Since when are American tourists banned?" he asked in confusion, and not just because of her words. Her scent... He couldn't place it beyond the light lily body mist she'd used.

"Stop playing dumb, puppy. You are breaking the treaty prohibiting unregistered Lycans in our territory."

The word Lycan widened his eyes. "How do you know what I am? And what are you?" Because her unique aroma indicated something other than human or wolf. If he were to explain it to someone, her bouquet reminded him of a finely aged wine. Something to be savored.

"You don't know?" She cocked her head. "Did no one warn you to stay away?"

"I'm kind of new to the wolf thing and having a hard time finding a place to settle in."

"Have you not met any others of your kind?"

"Yes. That is, I've talked to a few dudes in charge of wolf Packs, and we weren't a good fit. Which is annoying 'cause I'm not looking for anything complicated. I just want a place I can work on cars in peace." He babbled for no other reason than she kept staring.

The longest, thickest lashes blinked at him. "Who was your maker?"

"We called him Scarecrow. He's dead," Brock quickly added. "He didn't manage to escape unscathed from the prison we were in. Which is where he was forced to bite us, by the way."

Her turn to widen her eyes, the only thing visible given the hood also draped over most of her face. "Were you not chosen by a Pack alpha?"

"Nope, bitten in a filthy prison with terrible food. Do not recommend." He grimaced.

"How long ago?"

"Coming up on two years."

She strayed closer. "A lone wolf and you've survived this long. Fascinating."

"What are you?" he boldly asked, given she oozed danger. Yet he didn't see a single weapon on her.

"I am none of your business, puppy."

"A little bit old to be called pup, *ma'am*." He inflected the latter.

"Actually, the title is lady."

"In the presence of royalty. I am honored." He sketched a mock bow.

She pursed her lips. "I've never tasted your kind before. Rumor has it werewolf are foul."

Being a man in his sexual prime, the word "tasted" went right to his groin. It led to him being a little crass. "Feel free to give me a blowjob if you're curious. If it helps, I bathed this afternoon."

She recoiled. "You would insult me and call me a whore?"

"You're the one talking about tasting. I'm just offering."

"What if I wanted to bite you elsewhere?" she purred, coming closer.

"Sounds kinky. I like it. But I should warn you, I don't know what will happen if I bite back."

"Nothing because our species are not compatible."

He eyed her. "Looks like we'd fit together just fine if you ask me."

"I didn't. Come here." She crooked a finger, and he closed the gap between them, surprised to find he towered over her by several inches. She had such presence.

"Kiss me," she ordered.

"Gonna take off your mask?" he asked.

"Why not? It's not as if you'll remember." She tugged it down, revealing a beautiful face, pale and smooth but for the scar. The ridged rope of it snaked its way from her jawline across her nose.

"Well, hello there, beautiful," he breathed.

"You only think that because you're enthralled."

"Fucking right I am." The woman drew him on a level he'd never experienced.

She sighed. "Kiss me."

He grabbed her and did as she commanded, pressing his lips to hers. They were cooler than expected, and yet that didn't stop the sensual shiver that coursed through him.

She opened her mouth, and their tongues twined. Sharper-than-expected canines dragged over his tongue, and he shuddered. Those lips then dragged down his jaw to his neck, sucking the skin. He barely felt the pinch when she bit him, but he felt each sucking tug as if she had her lips on his dick.

He throbbed. Almost whimpered, and when she finally let go, he just about collapsed.

"Wow, that was fucking intense." Being a man who believed in giving as much as receiving, he dropped to his knees, his hands on her hips.

She sounded surprised as she gasped, "What are you doing?"

"You tasted me. Now I'm tasting you." His hands tugged down the leather that clung to her curves, revealing pale skin and only a thin patch of hair on her mound, dark like that on her head.

He kept tugging her pants until he could bend her knees enough to get his face between those alabaster thighs. At his first lick, she stiffened, only to soften as he teased her, tasted her, reveled in the flavor of this woman who was more than just a woman.

Who knew a lady would taste so... Not sweet, that was for the ordinary. The honey of this beauty was complex. Intoxicating.

When she came, hitching and crying out, her sex clenched the fingers fucking her, her honey a slick gush. He was completely ready to make her his.

He stood, a hand on his belt buckle to see her looking startled. Her full lips parted. "You should go now."

"Or you could get over here and come a second time." He crooked a finger as his other hand undid his pants and pulled free his hard cock.

She looked at it, then him, then shook her head. "This was a bad idea, puppy. You'll forget we ever met. You will leave London tonight and never return." She tugged up her pants and replaced her face mask while he stood there slightly dazed, her commands ringing in his head.

He struggled even after she left, a part of him demanding he go, but a bigger part of him wanted to stay. The lady—who never did give him a name—might not be a wolf, but she sure was interesting for a vampire.

Bite on his neck. Came out at night. Had his mind all messed up. She fit the bill. And he wanted to see her again.

Which was why when a request arrived out of the blue from somebody called Rick with the Cabal that governed Lycans, asking him if he'd like a job working for the Vampires led by Lord Augustus, he said yes. Came face to mask with the lady from the clock tower, name of Arianna, only she acted as if they'd never met.

Pretended she hadn't come on his tongue.

And being a man with too much pride, he faked it right back.

Until he couldn't do it anymore.

1

A DECADE later in a garage in London, a few days after Brock's friend, Quinn, left for Romania...

IT TOOK hours of work and a full jug of cleanser to restore the leather seats in the sportster. An added expense Brock wouldn't be paid for. Then again, the monster blood spilled all over Lady Arianna's car kind of was his fault.

In his defense, when they decapitated the attacking creature, they had no idea it would choose to croak and spill its blood all over the buttery leather. He'd had no idea why it attacked, or even what the fuck it was supposed to be. Although he did have to wonder if it tied into Quinn's secret mission. After all, the attack occurred during his old friend's visit.

Worse, Lady Arianna arrived while the gore still gleamed fresh. In good news, she didn't order his death. She was good at ignoring things. She still had yet to mention their moment in Big Ben. More than ten years and counting.

In the beginning, Brock thought it a reflection on his oral skills, only to realize she was just stuck up and arrogant. She thought Brock—whom she always called puppy—beneath her vampire, I'm-such-a-princess ass.

Her loss. He'd consoled himself with other women since. He really hated that none of them could compare. It might explain his dry spell. Five years, or was it going on six? He didn't really remember.

His lack of interest in the opposite sex explained why he spent more time than was normal in his garage, fixing cars. The sportster in particular got an uneven share of his attention. If asked, he would have blamed it on the demanding Lady Arianna, constantly showing up to harass him. And when she didn't, he would text and send her pics and questions until she did. He'd miss that now that the job was over. Or would she find him another car to restore? This was, after all, their fourth project together.

The monster blood had been painstakingly cleaned. The leather shone. The carpets were like new. Ready for the princess to sit her sexy, tight ass. Ten years, and he still got a flutter in the chest thinking of her.

Attraction should have been easy to fight. She showed him nothing but disdain. Tell that to his dick every time she came around. Must be some kind of vampy pheromone thing. Perhaps a drug in her nectar that made him moon over her, no better than a dog waiting for attention from its mistress. A mistress he was in tune with to an annoying degree.

Take now, for instance. He knew the moment she entered the building, although he always pretended he had no clue. He didn't want her knowing the effect she had on him.

"Hello, puppy. Have you fixed my car yet? Or have you inconsiderately killed another beast inside it?"

He didn't turn to look as he rubbed a rag on her hood to remove a single speck of dust. "Hey, princess, thought I smelled something spoiled." He'd long ago stopped calling her lady. And while she had to know princess was a jab, she accepted it.

"Surprised you smell anything at all given you've been out in the rain. Wet dogs really shouldn't be allowed inside." The derision in her tone should have roused his annoyance, but her rapier wit oddly enthralled.

"Is this your way of saying you're sorry you missed

me showering?" He grinned at her over his shoulder as he slicked back his still damp hair.

"You just want someone to blame for the hair clogging the drain," was her dry reply.

"Are you saying if I shaved, you'd change your mind?"

"Did you run out of batteries for your inflatable doll?" She hadn't missed a beat when of late he'd been getting a little more risqué with his taunts.

He burst out laughing. "Damn it all. I knew I should have paid extra and gotten the rechargeable version."

"It's been a money saver with my vibrator."

Too late she saw how she walked into it, and he dove. "Any time you need the real thing, just let me know." He winked. With her mask, he couldn't see her facial reply. Did she blush?

Doubtful. Lady Arianna was always cool and in control. Except for that one time in the clock tower...

"If you're done being a male, I have a question for you."

"I'm yours. Anytime. Anywhere. Although, if we have sex in your car, I might need an extra day to clean again. I get the feeling you're a gusher." He knew it for a fact.

"Thanks for confirming you're a crotch-licking canine. Can we move on?"

No, because he wanted closure. Why did she continue to pretend nothing had happened? And why had he let her get away with it so long?

It didn't used to bother him. But that was before he'd heard her name tied to that of Luis Garcia, a prominent Vampire Lord for another flock in Spain. Rumor had it they would be getting engaged before Christmas. It bothered him.

A lot.

"So what did you want to ask me?" he asked, walking away from her to drop his cloth into a bucket for the wash.

"Can you keep your mouth shut?"

She couldn't see the wry twist of his lips as he replied, "Tighter than a nun clamps her thighs."

"I've known some nuns. They're not all that pious."

That had him chuckling. "Listen, princess, if you want my word, then you know it's good." After all, he'd been working for her father, Lord Augustus, a long time now. He liked to think he'd earned the flock's trust.

"You can't tell anyone, not even my father."

The latter caught his attention. "Is something wrong?"

"Maybe. I'm not sure yet, but I don't want him going off on a rampage before I find out more."

"That bad?"

"It's related to the monsters we've been seeing in the city."

The monsters she spoke of were some hideous mishmash of bat, wolf, and dead things. They'd been killing baby vamps for months now. He'd encountered one recently in his garage even.

"You need a big strong man to protect you?" He ducked the moment he said it, expecting her to throw something to remove his head.

She sighed. "Can you be serious for just one moment?"

"Must be bad if you're coming to me for help. I thought us dogs weren't good for anything but sniffing assholes."

"I'm glad you mentioned sniffing, because that's exactly what I need from you."

He clutched his chest. "At last, the princess admits I am good for something. It's too much. I think I might die."

She snapped, "I'm going into the sewer hunting monsters. You in?"

He stupidly said, "Hell yeah." And then added a condition. "But only if you'll go on a date with me after."

She went still, the kind of stillness that made her such a good predator. If anyone but Brock closed their eyes, they'd never know she was there. Him? He had a sixth sense when it came to Arianna.

"This is a serious matter."

"Yup, and it's got a price. You. Me. Dinner and a movie."

"I don't eat in public."

He was aware she never took off her mask with people around. "I know. Dinner will be at my place. The movie on my projector screen sitting on my couch."

"Going all out."

"I was thinking it was more about respecting the fact you might not want your friends to see you with a dog." He winked.

"I'd rather skip the dinner part. I'm a vampire. I don't need food."

"But I know you enjoy it." With Vampires, blood provided a different kind of digestion. And she did eat regular food; she just didn't want to take off her mask. For a woman oozing confidence, she was awfully self-conscious about her scar. Then again, having been around Vampires for ten years now, he knew how judgmental they could be. It didn't help that he couldn't exactly tell her he didn't mind and that he'd seen it before. As far as she knew, he remembered nothing of their first encounter.

Her lips pursed. "Why are insisting on this? You know I'm dating someone."

"Dating, not married, making you fair game."

"You don't even like me," she pointed out.

"If I didn't like you, I wouldn't be asking you on a date. So?"

She stared at him and took a long moment before replying, "Fine. You have a deal."

2

WHAT HAD POSSESSED her to agree to a date? And with Brock of all people?

The man discomfited. Had from the day they'd met in that clock tower. A day she'd been taken off guard. Arianna had ignored all the warnings and drunk his blood. She'd been high with pleasure when he'd gone down on her. She, who thought herself cold and passionless, came on his tongue and fingers.

Almost fucked him like an animal then and there.

Was it any wonder she'd told him to forget? She'd whammied him, and yet there were moments when he looked at her... It was as if he remembered.

Impossible. Her mesmerizing skills were second only to her father's. No man, woman, or Lycan could resist. Hell, even most vamps couldn't prevail against her when she put her focus on them.

At times, she thought about repeating that moment. Reliving the ecstasy she'd not since been able to repeat. But the rules were clear. Vampires and Lycans could not mix. Whether for biological reasons or because of an old treaty, she didn't know or care.

She had no interest in being with Brock. Why, she was practically engaged. Now if only she didn't feel disappointed in the whole idea.

"When are we going hunting?" Brock didn't ask questions like why. He went straight to the point.

"Is now too soon? Perhaps you have a defleaing appointment?" She couldn't help but taunt. They'd been doing this since meeting. People assumed they hated each other. Good. It wouldn't do for a royal in the family to be thought to be consorting with a wolf. Her father would have a fit. Although she had often wondered, why? The rumor about them tasting foul? False. His remained the tastiest blood she'd ever had.

"Don't worry, princess. I'm up to date on all my shots. Just let me grab a few things and we can go."

While he gathered those items, she ran her hand over the car she'd had him restore. Now that it was done, she'd have no reason to visit. A good thing the garage at the mansion was huge. Might be time to find another project she could harass him over.

He clattered down the stairs from his loft apartment, carrying a knapsack, a rifle, and goggles with a light.

She arched a brow. "I thought your kind had decent night vision."

"Decent, yes, but in a sewer, I'd rather have a little something extra. Which reminds me." He grabbed an ankle-length leather duster from a hook and swirled it on. "Now I'm ready."

So was she. Any other man and she'd have taken him right then and there against the car.

Resist. She'd been doing it ten years already, but of late, it was getting more difficult. It didn't help it had been years since she'd been intimate with anyone. It didn't help no one could compare.

"I'm driving," she announced.

Unlike most men, he didn't argue. He just threw his things in the tight backseat and jumped into the passenger side.

The tight confines put her hand on the gear shifter close to his thick thigh. She almost licked her lips, remembering the taste of him. Maybe she should get it out of her system. Give him a good sucking, which would probably pale in comparison to the memory. She'd whammy him again and forget all about him.

What if he's better than I remember? What if, this time, I don't say no, and we have sex? What would happen if someone discovered she'd broken the rule against Lycans and Vampires?

He rumbled, "Waiting for something, princess?"

Did she have time to use his bathroom and rub one off? Even if she did, he'd smell it and know. It made her cranky as she growled, "Let's do this."

He pressed a button on a phone app, and the garage door clanked open. It shut behind the moment they exited.

The small roadster took to the road with a hum, handling the corners better than she'd imagined. Flowing easily as she drove them to the location she'd scouted out the night before.

Since he didn't ask any questions, she gave him a summarized rundown. "I tracked one of the monsters I wounded to a sewer outside this cemetery."

"I'm surprised you didn't go in after it."

"I had an event I couldn't miss." A ball hosted by her father, attended by her almost-fiancé, in front of the court.

"Do you think it's the entrance to the monster lair?"

"No."

He shot her a surprised look. "Then why are we checking it out?"

"Because I'd swear it wanted me to follow it."

"Those monsters aren't smart. The one I fought showed no signs of intelligence."

"Don't be so sure of that. I'm fairly confident it's lying in wait below, most likely with a few of its friends."

He arched a brow. "Care to explain why we'd intentionally walk into an ambush?"

"We aren't. The monster went in there." She pointed to the grate. "That's where it's probably watching. As for us? We'll enter the sewer a block away."

"You want to sneak up behind them and reverse ambush. I like it."

"No, the plan is to avoid them but to trace their scent back to where they entered the sewer."

"You do realize the sewer will make it almost impossible to smell anything of value."

"What happened to a dog's nose being able to decipher numerous scents at once?"

"I'd rather not be sniffing shit to find monsters when we could just flush them out instead and follow them when they flee."

She stared at him. "Flush them how?"

He grinned. "Easily. We just need to buy some skinny bottles of booze, a few rags, and a lighter."

"You're going to Molotov cocktail them."

"Everyone hates fire, even our neighborhood

monsters I'll bet. Once they scatter, we pick one and follow."

"We'll pick two," she corrected. "One for each of us and double our chances."

"I don't think we should split up."

"Worried I won't be there to save you?" she cajoled.

"More like aware your father will crucify me if anything happens to you."

She patted his cheek. "Your concern is adorable and unnecessary. I can handle myself."

"Such a cocky princess." He shook his head.

"With reason. So stop slobbering over my magnificence and make me some alcohol bombs."

It didn't take long to assemble what they needed and set the plan in motion. While Brock heaved off the heavy grate, she lit and lobbed bottles down—four in total—before they bolted.

Flames exploded under the street, brightening the hole where they'd removed the grate. Squeals erupted, and the first hairy body came boiling out of the shaft.

"Moving north," she said.

"On it," Brock announced, taking off after it.

Another emerged and fled in the same direction.

Only two?

That surprised, hence why she veered and jogged for the grate she'd been thinking of using. She arrived in time to see it being pushed aside and another creature emerging, smelling of singed fur.

She shadowed it, ignoring the buzzing at her hip from her phone. The mutant creature led her on a merry chase. When they reached a residential area, its limber limbs and strength let it climb walls and run across rooftops. She had no problem following it. When it leaped down, she didn't hesitate.

A mistake.

She landed in a ring of monsters.

And they looked hungry.

3

SPLITTING up didn't sit well with Brock, but the
princess insisted, and so he loped after the first beast to
come out of the hole, only to realize another followed at
his heels. He ducked into a door frame, and the dumb
things ran past, leaving a putrid stench in its wake.

He continued tailing them until they entered an
alley. He paused before turning the corner then
frowned. The darkness couldn't entirely account for
the fact they appeared to have disappeared. Impossible.
He stepped into the narrow crevice and followed the
scent of the beasts until it vanished.

What the fuck?

A glance to either side showed closed metal doors,
locked, and not smelling of the creatures but rather the
humans that used them. They beasts had given him the
slip.

He immediately texted Princess, but no surprise she didn't answer. He jogged back in the direction he'd come, picking up her trail easily enough. She'd found a monster of her own to tail.

It proved too easy to follow, although when they went above ground, he jogged on the street, knowing this section of housing ended in a gap too wide to jump. Before he reached it, he heard the signs of a fight.

He didn't think but ran, veering into the alley, and caught the scene of chaos as five monsters converged on Arianna, swiping and snarling. Mostly they missed. The woman moved like liquid, flowing under swipes, jumping high enough to strike down with her blade and take a head. An arm. When she dropped to the ground in a sweep, someone got their ankles chopped.

He couldn't help but whine as she finished them without leaving him any to play with. "No fair. You could have saved me one."

"What happened to your pair?" she asked, wiping her blade on the hairy carcass at her feet.

"Vanished into thin air."

"Is that some gaslighting way of saying you lost them?" She stepped over a body and headed for him.

"I was like a hundred feet behind them and poof. I turned the corner, and they're gone." He exploded his hands. "One minute they're stinking up the alley, and the next it's like their scent turns off."

"Or becomes something else," she opined.

"What's that supposed to mean?" he asked with a frown.

"I'm surprised I have to spell it out to a Lycan."

His brows shot up. "They're not Lycan."

"Never said they were, but they could be shapeshifters."

He gaped. "I mean, it's possible...But...Er..." What she said made sense. He'd just never made the connection mostly because the monsters were...well... monsters. The only thing that didn't make sense with her theory was that there was a difference between a human scent, a shifted Lycan scent, and an unshifted one. He'd only smelled human in that alley. How could it be possible for a monster to so completely change that he couldn't scent the difference?

"Look at your poor brain melting down," she teased as she leaned on the wall by him and pulled out her phone. Her fingers flew as she typed.

He could guess the message. *Cleanup needed.* Not just of the bodies but any cameras watching too. London had a shitload of them all over.

When finished, she tucked her phone away and pushed off from the wall. He expected her to ditch him. Instead, she canted her head. "It's still early enough for that dinner."

"Now?" He might have squeaked.

"There is a place with excellent Brazilian take-out on the way to your garage."

Holy shit. She was serious.

"But the bodies..." He swept a hand.

"Will be taken to a secure location. I will study them later once they've been stripped and cleaned."

"Study?" The word slipped from him in query. "Aren't you burning them to avoid detection?"

"We were, but given they keep cropping up, no matter how many are killed, we've chosen to take a more active interest."

"There does seem to be more of them lately." He'd only ever encountered one before this group. In his garage when a friend visited, along with a doctor working for the Cabal. They'd helped dispatch it. Nasty bugger. He sure didn't want to catch what it had. He'd washed his hands solidly after touching it and wore gloves when handling the bloody mess it left.

"If they derive from a lycanthropy-type infection, then that means whoever is making them can continue to churn them out."

"And become nothing more than a mindless beast." At least when he went wolf, he remained aware and could control his actions. Yes, he still hunted, but he didn't kill willy-nilly. He took care where he ran furry and four-footed. He avoided humans and detection. "Seems like a shit kind of deal. Why would anyone agree?"

"Could be they didn't have a choice. Just like I have to wonder if perhaps the biter is possibly rabid, given its creations are rather mindless and violent."

"That would be pretty bad." In the Lycan world, it took an alpha to have enough of the Lycanthropy virus to change a person. It didn't always work. Some died. Some lived the same as before. A special few became. It was the same in the Vampire world too. It was part of what protected humanity. Being unable to propagate quickly and with certainty kept them from subjugating humans, whom they still needed.

"Indeed, it would be. So keep it to yourself."

"Sharing secrets? Why, princess, if this keeps up, I'll start to think you like me."

"I'm sure you'll chew too loudly during dinner and ensure that doesn't happen."

"I am noisy when I enjoy stuff." A blasé statement to make as they returned to her convertible. Given her small snort, she got the double entendre.

A panel van arrived as she opened her door. It blocked the mouth to the alley. The cleanup crew already?

She paid them no mind as she slid into her seat, but Brock paused. Then he was yelling, "Down!"

A gun fired before he'd finished the word. The fact Arianna could move fast meant she avoided most of the spraying bullets, but not all. He smelled blood. She slithered over the console to the passenger side, where he'd ducked. He'd already yanked open the door, giving her an exit. Once she spilled to the ground, he shut it, using it as an extra layer of protection from the bullets.

He could smell her wound but had no time to assess given the barrage of bullets. Semi-automatics, illegal in the UK, but that never stopped the criminals.

She hissed, "I fucking hate guns."

Vampires, like Lycans, preferred to hunt with their hands, making an exception for certain types of weapons that kept them close for the kill.

"Who are they?" he asked. The Vampires had many enemies, but someone willing to move openly in such brazen fashion?

"Let's go catch one," she offered on a feral note just as the bullets stopped. In the sudden silence, an engine roared.

So did Arianna as she stood to see the van speeding away. Not interested in killing them after all. A quick dash to the alley mouth showed their true purpose. They wanted the bodies.

But was the princess pissed?

Her tone sounded pleased as she entered the combat zone and said, "Someone was awfully desperate to make sure we didn't examine those corpses. They sprayed bleach all over so we couldn't get a sample. Here's to hoping some of the spatter on my leather will be enough."

A distant siren had him hustling her. "We better get going. Company is coming."

"Not that way." She zipped her leather jacket as they went down the alley, away from the demolished car. His poor baby. All those hours and the first day it went out, it got wrecked beyond repair.

They emerged onto a quieter street that would soon waken given the sirens and the ratcheting gossip exploding as people woke and gawked.

"Where to?" he asked, keeping an eye open for a taxi.

"Wasn't the deal your place for dinner?"

"You still want to do that?"

"Why not?"

He gaped at her. "You're injured."

"You don't say. I'll need a moment to freshen up when we get there."

She limped by his side as they walked away from the wakening neighborhood. The shrill wail of the police cars woke those who slept, terrified those who'd been listening and cowered indoors, but the ones he worried about most? Those filming what happened. Any chance no one caught him or Arianna on video?

Better hope not. Lord Augustus would be pissed.

"You're scowling," she remarked.

"Wondering if we're about to become the newest TikTok sensation."

She glanced over her shoulder, the masked face giving nothing away. "My alley fight shouldn't be an issue. Very little lighting and windows."

"The shooting was on the street. Between doorbell cams and regular surveillance..."

"You're fucked. Should have worn a mask," was her unhelpful taunt.

"I wouldn't be so cocky given your car is the one full of bullet holes."

"As if it's registered in my name," she offered with a laugh. "I'm in the clear no matter what. Really the only one who should worry is you. Here's to hoping the news runs your good side."

"You think I have a bad side?" he complained.

"Hard to tell under the rodent you insist on wearing on your chin."

"Guess that's a hint to shave." He stroked his beard. He'd been growing it out for Movember.

"If you save it, you'll probably have enough to stuff a pillow." She wavered on her feet.

"Princess, you okay?" His expression creased with concern.

"Just f—" She didn't finish her sentence. Arianna suddenly buckled, and he only barely caught her. The scent of her blood had been present since the shooting, but as he held her and noticed her sluggish heartbeat, he realized she'd been downplaying her injuries.

Fuck.

What was he supposed to do? Logic said drop her off at home. However, while he trusted Lord Augustus to care for his daughter, his court was another matter. He knew Arianna would hate being at their mercy. It left him only one choice, and where she'd been planning to go anyway.

His place.

4

ARIANNA REGAINED CONSCIOUSNESS, feeling sluggish and sore. It took only a moment to recall the shooting. Then panic as she realized she had no idea where she was. At least she found herself in the dark, a good thing since her internal body clock insisted it was midday.

Rather than thrash wildly, she glanced side to side, barely making out shapes. She appeared to be in a tent, despite the fact she never camped.

Her fingers clutched at a blanket. Not hers. Too scratchy to be the eight-hundred-thread-count bamboo she preferred. She did, however, recognize that doggy smell.

Brock must have brought her to his place when she fainted.

Fainted.

37

The shame of it.

And from a simple wound too. Okay, maybe two. She glanced down. She couldn't see, but she did feel. Two throbbing points. Bullet holes because she'd been ambushed.

"Fuck," she muttered aloud, only to hear a reply.

"Praise be, she's alive!" Brock sang.

"You won't be if you don't tell me what's happened. Where am I?" she grumbled.

"In the garage, and as you can see, heavily under wrap. Whatever you do, princess, don't come out. I've got you covered best as I can, but when I had the skylight put in, I wasn't thinking I'd eventually have my Vampire girlfriend staying over."

"Your what?" she exclaimed. "I agreed to a dinner. Nothing more." Maybe some more of his excellent oral and a bite, but she'd already planned to make him forget about it. If only she could do the same.

"Sorry to ruin your street cred by calling you my girlfriend, but I had to say something when your daddy called."

"You could have tried the truth." Her father would be livid.

"I did tell the truth about how you got jumped at then shot at. He was the one who ordered me to call you my girlfriend to protect you."

"From what?"

"You and I are internet famous, princess. And before you argue, while the world has no idea who you are, your daddy's people recognized us in that video."

"They might wrongly assume I'm weak and try to take advantage," she muttered, quickly seeing the merit in her father's lie.

If they knew she was here at Brock's because of injuries, they might try to remove her from the picture. However, if she was visiting her paramour, then they wouldn't dare because the cost in lives—for them—would be too high. At the same time, the rule against their kind fraternizing with Lycans created its own set of problems, which she'd have to deal with later. She could already hear the cruel jests. *"Dog lover." "From behind must be the only way he can keep it hard." "Did you have to bribe him with a T-bone?"* The flock and the court weren't a kind place, and while they would never dare insult Arianna to her face, they would gossip.

"Where's my sword?" She didn't feel it strapped to her body. She only rarely went unarmed especially since the incident that scarred her face.

"To your left. Knives are under the pillow. Your phone is there somewhere as well, but I bagged your clothes and had them sent to a lab."

"My father gave you the address?"

"No. I sent it to people I trust. Shit happened while you were passed out."

"You mean other than turning me into a laughing-stock for sleeping with a pet?" She'd have a hard time living it down. And then there was her almost-fiancé. How would Luis react? Would her father have to tell the truth to salvage the merger? Would Luis break things off?

Why didn't she care?

"Who you fuck might be important in the Vampire world, but meanwhile in the Lycan one, things kind of blew up at a village in Romania."

"And you're mentioning this because why?" she asked.

"Because that village was dealing with a mutant situation similar to ours. In their case, it was confirmed the monsters were shapeshifting. Seems they had some guy experimenting for years, creating something he called Lycan-Z, a wolfman with the ability to follow orders and even talk, created by injection."

"The monsters we've fought aren't verbal." She'd looked into their eyes and seen no signs of intelligence, and the smell when they died indicated something severely wrong with them.

"But the similarities seem more than coincidental."

"When you say blew up, do you mean figuratively or literally?"

"Remember Dr. Silver, that broad you met a few days ago when you tracked that monster to my place?" At her nod, he continued. "So she shows up in that town, starts poking her nose in things, and finds out they've been making Lycan babies."

"And the Cabal allowed it?" she hastily interjected. The Cabal, those governing the Lycan, forbade pregnancies for the simple fact most ended in a fatality. It took special conditions to safely birth a child, not something that was widely known given it was simpler to ban it altogether and instead bite prospects to keep their numbers at a certain level.

"More like they didn't know because a Cabal member was covering it up. Anyhow, this mad scientist named Sascha took Dr. Silver, thinking he could use her in an experiment, only Quinn and a bunch of others went to the rescue, killed a bunch of the wolf-men, and destroyed the lab Sascha was using."

"So this scientist is dead. Still don't see the reason for interest."

"One, the scientist escaped, and two, it just so happens he used to travel to the UK regularly."

That got her attention. "Meaning he might be behind our monster problem."

"Exactly."

"This scientist most likely had a backup site for his research."

EVE LANGLAIS

"Which the Cabal is looking into, but I wouldn't count on them too much." His lips twisted. "It appears they're having an internal struggle."

"It's been long overdue. Too many rulers cause chaos. I'm surprised it's taken this long for them to butt heads." With the flocks, each of them was self-governed by a Lord or Lady. No one above them. Although they did have an understanding that if a particular flock drew attention, the others would take action, aka depose the leader.

"Ah yes, because the dictator style is a much better option," he drawled.

"My father is fairer than most."

"Until he isn't."

"Care to critique his ruling style to his face?" she offered sweetly.

"That wouldn't be a very smart boyfriend thing to do if I'm currying his favor."

She gnashed your teeth. "I can't believe you couldn't come up with a better excuse for my presence here."

"Blame your dad, who, by the way, said to call him before you went anywhere."

"What time is it now?" she asked.

"Just after two in the afternoon. If you want to avoid getting crisped by the very bright sunny day, then you'll want to wait a few hours before popping out."

42

"So I can die of boredom and starvation instead?" she grumbled.

"Sounds like someone's hangry. Hold on. I can fix that."

She heard him clunking off then returning to huff, "Hide under the blanket for a sec while I crawl in with you."

Since she had no better option, she tugged the thick comforter over her head, keeping her hands tucked inside. With her already weak and in serious need of blood, a sunburn would only make her situation worse.

The rustle of fabric warned he penetrated her tent.

"Okay, we're good. You can come out now."

She emerged to find him in the tent with her, bearing a lamp, which meant she could see him. "You shaved!" she exclaimed.

He rubbed his square jaw, clean of the beard he'd worn for years. "Since our incident went viral, I thought it best if I changed my look."

Speaking of look, a shirt covered her upper body and thighs, but she didn't feel any weight on her head. It led to her hands slapping her bare face. "My mask..."

"Was nasty so I removed it."

"You shouldn't have done that." She kept her face partially turned, her hair falling forward to hide the scar.

He reached and flicked it aside. "Don't hide on my account. You aren't the only one with scars. You should see the one on my thigh."

"Try being the only imperfect vampire," she retorted, only to wish she'd bitten her tongue.

"I take it you were injured before you were turned."

Everlasting perfection was the gift that came with vampirism. A body frozen in that moment in time. They healed without scar from almost every wound.

Almost being the key. Injured as young girl, she'd had to suffer because her father, who became Vampire while mother was pregnant with their youngest, refused to turn her until she reached a certain age.

"I'd rather not discuss it. What's that you've brought?" She noticed he'd lugged in a few items.

He held up a first aid kit. "Time to redress your wounds."

"I can do it myself."

"The front maybe, but the bullets also went through the back. So why not stifle the complaints and let me change the bandage."

"Fine." She lifted the hem of the shirt to bare her torso, feeling the twinge of her wounds, more than she should have after a healing sleep.

He kept his gaze serious and focused on the gauze that he peeled. He wiped her wounds with an antiseptic before retaping fresh bandages on them. "Turn around," he ordered.

She shifted on her bottom to give him access to her back.

He repeated the steps at the back, finishing with, "You're not healing."

"Because I'm hungry."

"I've got something for that." He handed her a bottle over her shoulder.

She grabbed it and frowned, reading the label. "A protein shake?"

"Yup, with extra iron. Thought you could use some given the blood loss."

"What I need is actual blood." She'd lost too much to heal. Hunger gnawed at her insides.

"Okay. Guess I'd better drink this then." She didn't understand what he meant until he snatched the bottle and started chugging the protein drink while holding out his arm.

"I am not biting you," she exclaimed, even as her mouth watered. Surely he wasn't as delicious as she remembered? As for the fact no one had tasted good since that one bite she'd had from him, she blamed it on a lack of appetite. As Vampires aged, the hunger lessened.

"Why can't you bite me?"

"For one, you're not on the menu. I've got plenty of donors at home."

"You're not currently home, though."

"It's not allowed."

"I won't tell."

"I've heard dogs taste bad." Which she knew to be a lie.

He shook his head. "Suck it up, princess. We both know you need it."

"I'll be fine," she insisted. A little weak, but that wasn't anything new given her lack of interest in plasma most days.

"So stubborn," he grumbled. "Eat." He pulled a pen knife and slashed. The deep cut welled with blood.

She turned away.

He clucked.

That earned him a glare.

He had the nerve to grin. "Come on, princess. You know you want to."

The temptation proved to be too much.

She grabbed his arm and sucked. Oh god, did he taste good. As rich as she remembered. Tickling all her pleasure spots. Intoxicating her. She finished with a groan of pleasure and flopped onto the bed.

"Damn, princess. I don't think I've ever made a woman feel that good."

She cracked open an eye. "You really aren't amusing."

"Says the woman who can't stay away from my garage. It's okay. I get it. I am a stud. The forbidden wolf fruit."

"I don't know why I bother talking to you."

"Because I don't blow smoke up your delectable ass."

"Don't be looking at my ass," she retorted even as she inwardly preened.

"You're the one always wearing butt-molding leather, which is like every man's wet fantasy."

"Until the mask comes off." She snorted.

"Please. That scar gives you character. It's sexy as fuck."

"I can see why the military discharged you. Banged your head one too many times."

His laughter filled the tented space. "Oh, princess, you are a delight."

Not a phrase usually used in conjunction with her. Surly. Bitchy. Arrogant. Cunt. And yet a decade later and this one man still joked and smiled and called her sexy. She had to fight his damned allure, so she changed the subject. "We should talk about what happened last night."

"Ah yes, the ambush. While you were napping, I did some digging. The van that took the bodies and had those creeps shooting at us was found abandoned by a bridge. It had been set on fire, I should add. We can forget any trace evidence. The CCTVs in the area caught four people. Two went into the alley; the other two were trying to make us into Swiss cheese."

"Any facial recognition?"

"Nope. All of them wore animal heads."

"Er, what?" She startled at the last bit.

"Not real ones. Halloween-type shit. Hold on, I'll show you." He rummaged on the other side of the tent bed, handing over a crinkly bag of chips and a bottle of cola—both her favorite kind. As he snared a laptop and logged in, she crunched on salty and smoking-hot buffalo chips and looked around. Sheets crisscrossed, tied to the ceiling and tucked under the king-sized mattress she sat on. It smelled of Brock. He must have dragged it down and tucked it under his loft. A good thing. His skylight would have toasted her otherwise.

"Here you go." He scooted closer with the laptop. "This is the footage going viral."

She munched some more, trying to ignore how he leaned close enough she could have turned her head to kiss him. For him it would be like the first time. For her? She'd been comparing every kiss since to it. They'd all been seriously lacking.

"There they are." He paused the video so she could see the driver emerge from the van along with his gang.

A lion, a bear, a rat, and— "Who the fuck wears an ostrich head to a shootout and body snatch?"

"They came prepared." His grim observation.

"More like they were waiting to clean up the results of the ambush."

He made a noise. "Ambush? That was barely a warmup for you."

"Me, yes. Anyone else would have been their dinner." They'd been losing the younger vamps to the monsters in high enough numbers that her father had ordered them not to leave the compound unless they were either in a group of three or more or with one of the older flock members. Many of them chafed at the change. The young did like their club parties.

"I wonder why they were so desperate to take the bodies," he asked as the footage finished with the van speeding off.

"That's the wrong question." She pointed to the picture of them, barely visible in another video, hiding behind the poor convertible. "Why leave us alive?"

"Doesn't look like they intended to, or did you miss the bullets flying?" he said sarcastically.

"If they were serious about us dying, they would have approached, guns blazing, until we had nowhere to run."

"Maybe they ran out of ammo."

49

"I'm thinking they were more interested in keeping us pinned down while they cleared out the bodies."

"Seems kind of drastic. Especially since they tried to ambush you. Wouldn't they have tried to finish the job?"

A good point that had her frowning. "Maybe you should stop arguing. It's ruining my buzz."

He quirked his lips. "Need another bite?"

"You need time to recover."

"I'm not human, princess. I can handle it."

"I'm fine." She could already feel the wounds knitting together, reacting to the potent infusion. She really had to wonder at the rumor of Lycan blood being shitty, given she'd never felt more energized, and she'd not even fed overly long.

"Maybe now you're okay, but you had me worried," he admitted. "I'm just glad I was there to catch you when you dropped."

Being rescued, what a novelty. The only other person who'd saved her from harm was her father.

"Thank you. I might have died without your intervention." An apology she could give because he wouldn't remember. She'd be making him forget this entire conversation because she couldn't have him recalling her like this. Weak. Imperfect. "You said my father wanted to speak with me."

"And only him," he added as he handed over the

phone pulled from his pocket. "He's got some of his human henchmen watching the garage outside."

That arched her brow. The flock Lord wouldn't have sent anyone unless he worried for her safety.

"Could I have some privacy?"

"You do realize I can hear you no matter where I am in the garage, right?"

"Then go outside." She waved a hand imperiously.

"Don't push it, princess."

"Can you at least pretend you're not insubordinate?"

"Sure, I'm good at that," he muttered enigmatically, sliding over to the edge of the tent. "Cover yourself. I'm going out."

"I'll be fine," she grumbled at his mollycoddling.

He left, and the cozy tent felt huge and empty without him. She really must have been weak to feel this way. Perhaps she should put a reminder in her phone to drink blood more often. At the same time, she should audition some new humans for the stable, someone with a flavor she actually enjoyed.

Like Brock's. Was it his Lycan heritage that made him so yummy?

She dialed her father's number, knowing it by heart. She never saved it in any contacts, nor did her phone keep it in its recent calls. This was her direct line to him.

He answered with a brusque, "You are in danger."

Because she loved to bug her dad, she replied, "I swear the dog has been nothing but a gentleman."

"Don't play with me, Nina." Her father used her nickname. "You can trust Brock, but no one else. Last night, a court member was attacked as part of a blackmail attempt."

That had her stiffening and yelling, "What? Who? Did you pay?"

"The ransom demand was for you, idiot," her father huffed. "Only they were premature given you escaped the trap to capture you. That text you sent me came at a most opportune time."

"Son of a bitch. Who sent the ransom demand?"

"I kind of decapitated the messenger." He sounded almost apologetic. "By the time I realized you were fine, I couldn't glue him back."

"What have we said about making zombies?" she chided. A skill thankfully only her father had. Necromancy was the power of only the strongest Vampires.

"I didn't bring it back to life, mostly because I doubted the monster could have said much."

"Wait, they sent the ransom demand with a monster?"

"Yes. And before you ask, I had it transported to the lab."

"Excellent."

"It was ambushed en route."

"Fucking seriously?" she shouted.

"Language, Nina."

She rolled her eyes. "Kind of warranted, but whatever. Any other news?"

"Other than the fact last night was a targeted attempt at using you to manipulate me?"

"Not a very good one," she complained. "They would have sent more to ambush me if I was a guy."

"If it makes you feel better, they placed enough value on you that they expected me to hand over control of the flock in exchange."

She laughed. "Wow, guess they know your weakness." Because her father would have done it to save her.

"Not funny, Nina." He grumbled her familiar nickname. "I won't have people threatening my daughter. It makes me look weak." The last time she'd been attacked and left for dead with a slashed face, her father went scorched earth, and an entire flock, down to the people who fed them blood, was eradicated.

"Who do you want me to kill?" she asked because such a slight could not go unpunished.

"I don't know."

"I'll find them." Her dark promise.

"No, you will not. We don't know what we're facing yet, and I won't have you walking into a trap."

"I escaped from their attempt relatively unscathed."

"Meaning the next one won't be as easy. We need to be ready, which is why you need to lie low for a few days, maybe a few weeks, while I get a handle on things."

"Weeks?" she complained. "Where exactly am I supposed to go?"

"I have an idea for that, actually. Hold on a minute." He put her on hold. She drummed her fingers as she heard Brock in the distance talking to someone that involved lots of, "Yes, sir."

The line to her father clicked open. "It's been taken care of. At nightfall, Brock will remove you from your current location to a safehouse in the country."

"I'm sure he's got better things to do than chauffeur me around."

"He's already agreed. And he'll stick with you until I give the all-clear."

"I am not hiding in the country while you hunt down the enemy," she hissed.

"It's not hiding. It's you recovering and getting strong again so that when I do find out who's behind it, I can send in my best warrior to handle it."

When he put it that way...

"You do realize if I go on a fake holiday with the dog, your court is going to run with the news."

"How many times have I told you words don't matter?"

She fingered her scar. Maybe for him they didn't. For her, they reminded her of when she'd failed. It wasn't just her attacked that day, but her other two siblings. Her older brother—a week from his twenty-first birthday and the change—cut to pieces. Her younger sister felled in her crib. She couldn't bear to remember what happened to Mother. Arianna only escaped with her life because they weren't done when her father arrived and, with a mighty fury, killed everything in sight.

Every time someone in the court whispered about the mark on her flesh, it was as if they pointed a finger. Maybe if she'd woken sooner instead of when they attacked her in bed... Fought harder...

"Nina..." Her father's tone softened. "I need you to be safe."

His fear at losing his only child was the only reason she agreed. "Very well, I'll go to this safehouse."

To which Brock yelled, "Road trip!"

5

When Lord Augustus called—while still on the phone with his daughter—and asked Brock to watch over Arianna, he didn't hesitate.

"Don't worry. I'll guard her with my life."

"I know you will. But she won't make it easy." The mighty Vampire lord sighed.

"I'm aware of her stubborn side."

"My only concern is how she'll feed. I can't send any of our current options to the hideaway, or I might lead the enemy to her."

"Don't worry about the blood. I'll figure something out." He didn't admit he'd given her his. He knew the Vampires considered Lycans to be dirty. No better than drinking blood from a farm animal. Funny how Princess enjoyed it. She'd worn that afterglow that happened with good food—or sex.

"Keep her safe," was the lord's last request—and warning—before he hung up.

Brock rubbed his hands together in excitement. He and the princess, alone for a few days at the very least.

She yelled from her tent, "I can smell your smugness from here."

"Don't blame me for the fact you're daddy's little girl. Fear not, princess, the big bad wolf will keep you safe."

"The big bad wolf is gonna end up a rug if he doesn't stop annoying me," was her sweet riposte.

"Someone's a little grumpy. You need to suck on me again, princess? Or do you need a good shag? Is your fiancé not giving it to you often enough?"

"My sex life is none of your business," she hissed.

"So is that a yes to packing batteries for a dildo then?"

She growled

He grinned as he snared his bug-out bag from under the stairs to his loft. A former military guy with a secret, he was always ready to go. He didn't have anything suitable for Arianna, though. Her slim build compared to his stocky one meant pretty much only his shirts would fit her so he packed a few extra and more of the iron-fortified protein shakes.

"How are we getting to the country?" she asked. "The cars in your shop are in pieces."

"Motorcycle, princess."

"I've seen your bike. It's not meant for two," she huffed.

"Quinn and Silver managed to make it work."

"For a short distance," she retorted.

"And we'll only go a short way as well. I've got something a little more road-trip worthy we can swap into."

"Why don't you keep it here?"

"Because a smart man doesn't keep everything in one spot just in case shit goes sideways."

"Do you worry often about that happening?"

"Every single day." He went to war a naïve boy. Came back a changed man.

"I'm bored," she complained. "Is the sunlight really that bad?"

The afternoon waned, but his skylight still let in way too much brightness. "Give me a second. I've got an idea."

It involved a spray can of black rubber, a precarious stacking of chairs on his kitchen table, and him aiming for the window overhead. Only once he'd coated it did he leap down and do the same for the tiny windows in the roll-up door.

Hello, darkness. With no lights on, he could see only teeny pinpricks here and there where sunlight tried to penetrate. It should be good enough Princess wouldn't ignite into a pyre.

"I think you're good to come out now."

She emerged slowly, not the haughty and capable Vampire princess he'd come to know, but a softer-looking woman in his shirt, which hit her midthigh, with a sword down her back and a knife strapped to her thigh.

Fuck it was sexy.

"Is this good enough?" he asked. "You need me to try and stuff some of those cracks?" The garage door especially had issues where the weatherstripping had flattened.

"This is fine." Her gaze went to the bulging knapsack. "You weren't kidding about being ready. I've never had to flee anywhere before," she mused aloud.

"To be honest, me either, so this is a first for both of us."

She noticed her boots, cleaned of gore, on a workbench. "I thought you mailed off all my clothes for testing."

"Figured they had enough with the blood on the leather and fabric. And I know how annoying it is to break in new ones."

No mask meant he got to see a genuine smile as she slid them on her feet. Did she look ridiculous in his Ozzy T-shirt, boots, and bare legs?

Nope. She looked utterly dangerous to his poor fucking heart. It was long past time he admitted, if only to himself, he was in love with the princess. Ten years overdue. But never too late.

"I might need a coat if we don't want to cause a stir," she remarked, glancing at her outfit.

In the end, he layered her in an oversized hoodie emblazoned with the UK flag. He used it when he wanted to pass as a tourist in the crowd. For her bare legs, a pair of his track pants, cinched at the waist with rope. A baseball cap that she tucked her hair through, using it like an elastic, completed the ensemble.

She looked nothing like a princess.

She kept poking in his things enough that he finally asked, "What are you looking for?"

"Bandanna to cover my face. Surely you have something left over from the pandemic?"

"Covering your face will draw attention."

"So will this scar," she snapped.

"And you will be dismissed just as quick because no one will recognize you."

"I don't want anyone's pity."

"Why would they pity you? You're gorgeous and you know it, so stop fishing for compliments."

She gaped at him.

It was cute. He could see her getting ready to

argue, and given he was tired of pretending and acting aloof, he did something that might get him killed.

"I see you need proof. How's this?" He dragged her close and kissed her.

To his surprise, she didn't bite off his lip. She didn't do anything as he slanted his mouth over hers, and then there it was, a tentative nibble of his lips. It turned into a passionate embrace that he wanted to never end, only someone tried the door to his garage, rattling it in its frame.

It should be noted the only person who usually visited his place of business was the princess. With all his other Vampire clients, he arranged to pick up and drop off their vehicles elsewhere. Delivery people had a slot that led to a bin inside his shop.

Maybe it was those climate activists again. He'd taught a lesson to a trio of them a few weeks ago when he caught them spray painting his roll-up door with some message about cars killing the world. He made them scrub, sand, and repaint the whole damned thing.

He paused and they both turned their heads to stare. Whoever tried to open it didn't knock or call out.

"Can you smell who's out there?" she whispered.

He shook his head. He had the fumes from the spray can stuck in his nose. Nor did he have a camera watching because he'd not wanted to do anything that would make the princess feel uncomfortable dropping in for her visits. Vampires did not like being videoed.

"You said my father had some guards outside?"

At his nod, she fired a quick text off to someone. The reply pinched her lips. "My father just tried contacting Rico and his team. No answer."

"Maybe they're having afternoon tea," he suggested while not believing it. No way would Lord Augustus tolerate his employees shirking their responsibility.

"We need to leave."

"It's still daylight outside."

"I'm aware," she snapped as she tucked the hood of the sweatshirt up. It covered the neck and sides of her face. Leather gloves took care of her hands. Sunglasses a portion of her face. It still wasn't enough. The lower half of her visage remained exposed.

"Hold on, I have a better idea." The welding helmet he offered meant her removing the ballcap and glasses, but with the hood tucked over, she was protected. If odd looking. He'd take odd over barbecuing though.

The control panel for his regular door beeped and flashed red.

"They're trying to hack my lock," he huffed.

"Then we should get going."

He'd already strapped his bag to the rack on the

rear fender. He straddled it as the door beeped again. Wrong code.

She slid on the back of the bike as he started it, the rumble of the engine loud. It led to those at the door suddenly kicking at the panel as he gunned his machine. The bay door rattled up on the track, taking its sweet fucking time. It exposed them bit by bit, but he'd prepared for that. He aimed his revolver at the person with the rubber bear head dressed in black crouching to come through the widening gap.

Bang.

The intruder ducked back out but eerily didn't say a word. Not even to cry out in pain or warning.

The garage door was a few feet up and still climbing when the bullets sprayed from outside. The other door was smashed in, and a guy in a rooster mask stumbled inside.

"Fuck!" He and the princess dove off the machine and, with their two exits on that floor blocked, headed for the stairs and his loft.

Once there, he dove under his bed while she muttered, "Hiding under the mattress isn't exactly helpful."

"Don't be so sure." He squirmed back out holding a grappling hook and rope. "It's where I keep the best toys." He began to swirl the tined end. "Watch out just in case I miss," he warned before he tossed the tined contraption.

The first shot hit the skylight that he'd just had replaced the day before after that monster crashed through it. Glass tinkled as it rained down. He turned his head aside to avoid any in his face and gave his head a shake. He gripped the fallen grapple and tossed it again.

Clang. The hook caught on the edge of the hole and the rope dangled, drawing the attention of those on the ground floor, who'd fully entered and adjusted their aim higher.

"Get climbing." He slapped her ass, and she pursed her lips rather than move.

"Don't you dare get killed," she ordered.

"Why, princess, I didn't know you cared."

"You still owe me dinner and a movie." Her retort as she leaped for the rope and began climbing hand over hand, making herself a target. Not for long. He snared his rifle from the couch and stood on the edge of his loft.

"All right you pussies hiding behind a mask. Who's dying first?" He drew their attention and shot at them. Hit them a couple of times, not that you could tell given the bastards didn't even flinch.

Who and what the fuck were they?

"Clear," she yelled. "Move it, puppy."

"I'm coming, your bossiness." He grabbed the rope, only to hiss as a bullet singed over the back of his hand.

"Toss it up." Her voice was muffled from behind the helmet visor.

"What?"

"Your gun, moron."

Oh. He heaved the rifle and then ducked as the assholes below reloaded to start peppering the loft again. Princess didn't have a great angle for shooting them, so she aimed for other stuff instead, like the propane tank he used for his butane torch. It exploded in a ball of fire that stopped the bullets long enough for him to grab the rope and start shimmying his ass upward.

He was almost to the top when they started shooting again, searing his thigh, but it was the shot to the ass that had him yelping as he reached the rim and heaved himself over. "My ass!" he exclaimed. "Fuckers shot my ass."

"If we make it to the safe house alive, I'll kiss it better. Now move, puppy. Our reprieve won't last long." It didn't last at all, as their assailants had climbed to the loft and fired into the ceiling of the garage, punching holes in the roof.

As they ran across the roof with its slight peak, he huffed, "Long jump to the other side."

She soared across more gracefully than him. He hit the edge, teetered, and slammed forward with a grunt.

"Come on," she insisted when he struggled to pull his phone from a pocket.

"Just one second."

"Not time to be texting!"

"Trust me, you'll like this." He unlocked his phone using a special string of numbers. Then he grabbed her by the hand, yelling, "Run."

The explosion of his garage still caught them and slammed them flat.

Stunned, it took him a moment to realize Princess was struggling to breathe beside him because she was laughing so fucking hard.

6

"I CAN'T BELIEVE you blew it up!" Arianna exclaimed, looking back to see a smoldering ruin where his garage once sat.

"Told you I had a get-out plan."

"What's wrong, don't trust the flock?" she mocked.

"Do you?" he countered.

She offered him a toothy grin. "Nope. Where to now, Mr. Prepared for the Apocalypse?"

"Now we go for a long walk," he uttered with a grimace.

"Why would we do that when we can ride the tube?"

"You do realize there are cameras everywhere. We'll be seen."

"And long gone before they come looking. Come on." She led the way down from the roof. The sound of sirens already clamored as first responders raced to the scene of the explosion. They'd better escape this area fast before the terror squad locked down a perimeter.

The attack reinforced her father's warning about staying out of sight. Whoever this enemy was, they weren't being subtle. And she wasn't quite ready yet to take them on. Her wounds might be finally healing thanks to that delicious drink of Brock's blood, but that tiny sip only barely covered her hunger. She'd been running on so little for so long that her body protested. Hard to find the appetite to eat when nothing satisfied —until now. Brock satisfied her thirst in a way she didn't want to examine too closely. Not yet.

"I can't believe you're making me ride public transit," he complained.

"Too good to ride with the plebes?" she teased over her shoulder as they headed down out of the waning daylight. Thank goodness they were late enough in the year it would be dark soon.

She peeled off the welding helmet lest she draw attention and tossed it into a garbage can. They could stay underground until nightfall if needed.

Brock grabbed her hand, squeezing it tight. "You okay? Any new wounds?"

"Nah, I'm good, but you're not," she remarked. She could smell the blood. "I can help with that."

She dragged him into a washroom stinking of piss

and bleach, the old tile and grout never quite able to be clean of its messier patrons' habits. The stalls were heavily graffitied, but she ignored their messages as she closed the door.

"Pull down your pants."

"Now, princess, while I'd really love for you to blow me, now is not the time."

She grabbed his hand with its sluggish bleed from a bullet. She licked it, savoring the saltiness of his blood, laving it clean, and stopping it from leaking. "Coagulant in my saliva. Remember?"

"Oh." He then grinned. "Why didn't you just say you wanted to kiss my ass?"

"You make me wonder why I even bother trying to help."

"Because you can't resist my rugged charm."

She snorted. "Now you're pushing it."

He turned around as he undid his pants and slid them down, revealing tight black briefs with a rip in them wet with blood. He tugged them down as well to show off taut buttocks with a hole.

"I think the bullet is still in there. Don't freak out."

"Why-What-Jeezus, princess," he exclaimed as she latched onto his wound and sucked hard enough to draw out the metal and spit it to the side. Then she licked to stop the flow of blood. And while she was crouched, she did the same for the strip on his leg.

She stood and said, "All better?"

He groaned. "Not really."

"Did I miss a spot?" She hadn't sensed any other wounds.

He pulled up his pants. "Let's just say being around you is always painful."

No need to ask why. His desire filled the space. It even matched her own. A decade she'd spent pretending it didn't exist.

It was getting harder and harder to remember why. It couldn't be because she feared the flock's disapproval. They'd long disliked her for being imperfect and only tolerated her because of her father.

Her words emerged husky. "We need to go before they shut down the station." They'd already wasted precious minutes.

"If we must." His reply was full of disappointment.

A strange lightness filled her at his unabashed attraction. He saw her scar, and yet he wanted her in spite of it. Maybe he needed glasses?

Maybe she should have a little more faith in him and herself. Was it so impossible to believe he found her beautiful?

They raced to catch the next train. As the doors closed, she could see police in full SWAT gear jogging onto the platform. The train didn't move, and the doors slid open as an announcement told them to disembark and ready their identification.

"Fuck," he cursed.

"Follow me," she stated as they slid out, staying to the back of the crowd and sidling sideways. To anyone that looked, she caught their gaze and pushed a compulsion.

You saw nothing.

When they reached the end of the platform where a SWAT member stood guard to ensure no one escaped into the tunnels, she could have gnashed her teeth. His helmet made it harder for her to mesmerize him.

His walkie crackled. "Runner in the east end of the tunnel."

The opposite side from them.

The guard jogged away, and no one noticed them jumping down from the platform, Brock landing with a slight wince. He didn't complain.

They walked, flattening to the wall when the train did finally rocket past. No one seemed to notice their sudden arrival at the next station as they blended with the crowd exiting the train while those boarding pushed to get on. They disembarked and boarded a few times, changing routes, surely losing anyone who might have followed.

To her surprise, while a few people stared a little longer than they should at her face, no one said a word as they traversed London. The early evening hour meant they still had to contend with more people than she liked being around, and the smells... Would it kill some of these people to shower and use a deodorant?

She didn't realize Brock had a destination until he said, "Last train. We get off in two stops."

They boarded the packed tube. With one hand holding an upright pole, Brock provided a body shield that allowed her a little space between the support handle and the door on the opposite side. No one dared cross into the line of view, given his mighty scowl.

She might have thought him annoyed if not for his wink when an even darker look sent someone trying to home in on her space fleeing.

He mouthed, *You okay?*

She replied, "Still waiting for my dinner."

"I take it what I offered earlier didn't count?"

"You're lucky I didn't make you wear that protein drink."

"I was talking about the *wine*."

"Oh. That was okay."

He arched a brow and leaned close to whisper for her ears alone, "Looked more than okay to me."

"When you said dinner, I expected you to put on an apron and whip me up something American and greasy and delicious."

"Wait, you think I can cook?" He looked so utterly appalled she laughed.

The corner of his eyes crinkled and matched the smile on his lips. How had she forgotten that strong jaw under all that hair? And that mouth...

She crossed her legs and hoped the smell in the place masked her sudden recollection.

Judging by the flare of his nostrils, she most likely failed. He reached for her, his hand spanning the edge of her waist and drawing her close. "This is our stop."

They exited the crush of people onto a mostly empty platform. He dragged her into the first tunnel before spinning her against a wall and kissing her.

Damn him for being the only one to steal a vampire's breath.

She panted against his lips. "Shouldn't we be getting out of the city?"

"Yes. I blame you for being so distracting."

"I did nothing."

"Which is the problem," he grumbled, leaning away from her, but he kept a hand on her lower back as he guided her from the station into a less-than-savory section of the city. No wonder the station was empty. Once dark hit in these parts, smart folk stayed inside.

At the same time, it was also the perfect place for two people needing to hide. People in this neighborhood wouldn't be calling the cops and would only rat for the right price.

No one spared them a second look as they walked with purpose. Never hunch. Only victims curled in on themselves. Predators moved tall and proud, their every glance daring to give them a reason to act.

They only went a few blocks before he entered a rundown apartment building, the lock on the main door long busted by the looks of it. The elevator was out of service.

"This doesn't look like a storage unit," she remarked as he led her down some stairs.

"As if I'd keep my stuff somewhere ordinary," he teased.

The basement smelled of piss and machine oil, even a bit of death. Given the sewer access in the floor, not surprising. Thankfully they didn't descend into the smelly sewage tunnels. The basement led to another, someone having knocked through and shored up the space between the buildings. They traversed to find someone on the other side sitting on a ratty couch, watching a video on a tablet.

The guy with half his head shorn, the other a shocking neon green, didn't look up as he mumbled, "Pay up or fuck off."

"Nice to see you, too, Bobby."

A sullen gaze rose. "Well, shit, if it ain't the bearded man of fame."

"Don't know what you're talking about," Brock taunted. "I'm a former military man. We love a smooth jaw."

The guy snorted. "Can't believe you shaved it, mate."

"What can I say? My girlfriend says it tickles when I'm going downtown," Brock jested. The guy laughed, and she did her best to not punch them both.

"Making a withdrawal?" Bobby asked.

"Yup. I need to float the mini, ASAP."

Bobby tapped his tablet. "And you'll be paying how?"

"Don't suppose you'd give me credit until I come back with cash?"

Bobby had a wet chuckle at that query.

"You're killing me. My garage blew up with my safe," Brock complained.

"The mini ain't all you've got in storage. You know I've been eyeing those big wheels of yours."

"That Humvee was going to be my retirement project and is worth way more and you know it."

Bobby pulled out a wad of cash. "Since you're short... How about a deal?"

In the end, Brock negotiated for them to get a fat stack of bills, half of which he gave to Arianna. He also got a revolver out of the deal, which he strapped under his jacket. Then they left.

As they got out of sight and hearing of the grifter, she couldn't stop herself from asking, "What just happened? Where are we going?"

"The ferry."

"Why would we bother doing that?"

"Because that's where we'll be picking up our wheels. I have a deal with Bobby and his gang. Think of them as a different kind of storage unit, the kind that turns a blind eye."

"This is all very cloak and dagger. We could have just rented a car."

"Which leaves a paper trail, not to mention they all have those GPS things these days."

"So does your phone."

"Please, princess. My phone, like yours, isn't the kind mere mortals have." He smirked. "I don't even have a monthly bill for it."

"You sound awfully proud of that."

"Says the woman with no bills to pay."

She grinned. "Jealous?"

"Very. Bobby and his boys ain't cheap."

"And you trust them?"

"Hell no. Do I believe they'd snitch for money? Yes. So here's to hoping no one's offered anything yet."

"This escape is getting complicated," she observed.

"It just seems like that because I'm covering our tracks."

They made their way to the ferry, currently loading up cars and passengers, although not many as the evening waned. They threaded the parked cars, heading for a multi-color Mini Cooper that looked older than him. He reached under the rear wheel well and pulled out a magnetic key box.

"This is our ride?" She couldn't help sounding dubious. While it was well kept, each of the obviously replaced panels clean of rust, it didn't have the wow factor she'd expected from a guy who restored old cars for a living.

"Yup. Ordinary enough no one will pay her a second's notice. No nav system. Nothing. License plate is clean as a whistle."

"It's small."

"One of the few things I own that is," he said with a wink.

She sat in the passenger seat and watched him squeeze in. "Fucking short-ass Bobby." He cranked the seat back, and she noticed just how old the car was by the lack of electronics. Roll-down windows. Cassette deck.

"Is this like a Flintstone car requiring feet to move?" she only half joked.

"Shh, you'll hurt Janey's feelings."

"Janey?"

He patted her dash. "I named her after the woman who took my virginity. Worn around the edges but a solid ride."

She coughed despite the fact Vampires never got sick. When she recovered, she asked, "Did Bobby pack a picnic basket? I'm hungry."

"We'll be across the river and offloading shortly. But in the meantime, feel free snack on me."

"What?" A soft exclamation. "I am not biting you again."

He leaned in close, baring his neck. "I know you didn't take enough earlier."

"Too much and you'll be useless."

"I'm sturdier than you think, princess. And I need you strong too."

She wanted to resist, to say no, but that taut flesh teased. The flutter of his pulse made her mouth water. His hand rested on her thigh as he cajoled, "Come on, princess, have a bite."

"People will see."

"They'll see a couple making out and steaming up the windows."

"I'm a vampire. We don't get hot."

"Is that a challenge? What if I touch you?" His hand slid to the seam of her pants and caused her to quiver.

Her lips parted. "This isn't the time for distraction."

"Then stop arguing and take what you need." He pressed on her, and she gasped before letting herself kiss the skin of his throat.

The tiny lick tasted of salt. The bite she couldn't help broke skin and gave access to ambrosia.

Drinking blood was pleasant, but sucking on Brock? Pure pleasure. It wasn't just the flavor of him that enticed but the way he didn't completely turn slack-jawed and drooling. He stroked her. First over the pants she'd borrowed then sliding his hand past the waistband to finger her.

Damn but it felt good. He rubbed while she sucked, her hips rolling to his pressure, her moans against his flesh making him shiver and groan in reply.

When she came, she yelled against his neck before licking it to stop the blood. She leaned back in her seat, sated in so many ways.

And he was right. The windows were too steamy to see inside.

7

Princess tried to whammy him before the ferry docked.

"You won't remember me biting you. Nor will you ask me again. And no more kissing or touching. You will forget that happened too." She stared him in the face.

He stared back.

"Do you understand?"

"Loud and clear, princess." She still wanted to play games. He knew a game too. It was called "let her think it worked." For now. Once they were alone, though, it would be long past time for some honesty.

The ferry docked, and they drove off, just one of many cars weaving the London streets. They made it to the edge of the city before her phone rang.

She answered it with a sweet, "Yes, Daddy?"

Didn't need super hearing to hear the hollered, "Did it occur to you to notify me you were alive? When I heard the garage blew up, I thought you were inside!"

"Surprise, I'm not."

"Not funny, Nina!" Lord Augustus still bellowed. "You could have called."

"We've been kind of busy. What with escaping the hit squad that came after us. What happened to our protection?"

"Rico and his crew are dead. The reports filtering out have Brock as some kind of chop shop that got caught in the crossfire. Given the viral video of the two of you getting shot at, the police are calling it gang violence."

Well, that was offensive. He didn't deal in black market parts. Most of the time.

"Oh, it was a gang all right. The same group of mask-wearing assholes that shot at me last night. Only this time they came guns blazing. *In daylight,*" she emphasized.

"Trying to get you while you're vulnerable," her father grumbled. "Bastards. Are you out of the city yet?"

"Almost." She side-eyed Brock. "We had to take a circuitous route to ensure we weren't followed."

"Tell Brock to not go to the lodge. At this point I'm worried it's been compromised."

She glanced at Brock. "You heard that?"

"Yup, and if it's any consolation, I had already decided to avoid it."

"So where are we going?" she asked him.

To which Lord Augustus exclaimed, "Don't say it. I don't want to know in case I have some traitors in my court."

"In case?" she taunted. "I think we both know there are a few that would gladly plot your demise." Not because Augustus was a shitty leader but because he actually led, meaning those who wanted to be bad couldn't.

Her father uttered a sound that would have made most throw themselves to the ground, begging forgiveness. "This isn't amusing, Nina. They dared to come after you."

"And failed, Daddy."

"They'll pay for it," he promised darkly before hanging up.

Brock chuckled. "He'll make a formidable father in-law."

"Why? Because my husband will have to treat me nice as opposed to the chattel he bargained for?"

He winced. "Ouch. I'm surprised your father

would wheel and deal for you, given how much he appears to value you."

"Oh, he would never. I'm the one who angled for this merger between the families. I've always wanted to holiday in Spain." Where Luis was based. Vampires had even stricter rules than Lycans when it came to territory. As in, most didn't allow entry unless by invitation for a specific event.

"I don't know if I could marry for anything less than love," he admitted.

"Love?" She snorted. "A fleeting emotion."

"Is it?"

"What would you know? You've been single since you started working for my father."

"I've dated," he defended.

"Barely."

"Why, princess, have you been keeping track of my love life?"

"As the only Lycan in our territory, I wanted to make sure you weren't involved with anyone that might cause the flock harm."

"That's pretty weak given I only date humans."

"We haven't just been monitoring your paramours but also all your known associates. There was concern in the court that you might start creating Lycans to form a Pack."

"That's way too many people to deal with. No thanks."

"Some worried you might breed children." The Lycan Cabal forbid it, not only because it was very dangerous but also to keep a stranglehold on their power.

"Never had an interest, and it's no longer even possible given I got the big snip."

"There's invitro."

He cast her a glance. "Still no. You've seen how I live. I'd have a hard time convincing a woman to stick around, never mind taking the chance the pregnancy would kill her."

"There are ways to make the birth successful."

"So I've heard. Quinn says he and his doctor friend stumbled upon a village that's been having babies for a while. And that turned into a clusterfuck by the sounds of it."

"Never wanted a Brock Junior?" she teased.

"Ever wanted a mini you?"

"Never!" she uttered, somewhat appalled. Only to also admit, "Usually it's encouraged we have a few before the change. However, seeing how my father suffered when my mother and siblings were killed made me decide against it. That was the night my grandfather also lost his life and my father became Lord."

"I didn't know."

Her lips turned down. "Because it's not something I speak about. They died the same night I got this." She fingered her scar. "My younger sister was only seven."

"I'm sorry."

"Those who dared certainly regretted it. My father eliminated every single person associated with the flock that thought they could attack us."

"Jeezus, that's brutal."

"You don't approve?"

"I do. I just can't believe anyone was stupid enough to attack your family like that. They totally deserved what they got."

Her lips curved. "Total annihilation is a good way of ensuring it never happens again."

"What's it like growing up with a Vampire as a dad? Did you go to a regular school?"

"I did until the attack. Then I learned via tutors."

"What about friendships?"

"I never had many to start with. Just a few from when I did dance and played the violin."

"You play an instrument? I would have never guessed."

"Because everyone likes to assume all Vampires are bloodthirsty beings only into debauchery. I can't blame you. Movies and literature haven't exactly been kind."

"It doesn't help that some flocks actually do

embrace that image, but I was thinking more along the lines that I wouldn't have thought you were into noncontact arts because you're so good with weapons and fighting."

Her lips twisted. "My skills in battle didn't come until after I lost most of my family. Being almost killed left its mark. I was determined never to be so weak again."

"If it helps, I doubt anyone would ever accuse you of that."

"And yet here we are with enemies once more brazenly attacking."

"You think it's flock-related?" Brock asked.

"Didn't my father tell you about the ransom attempt?"

"Yeah, I just have a hard time believing anybody would be that stupid. I mean anyone who's watched you at all can see you're dangerous."

She laughed. "People are so in awe of my father they don't look to see who actually helps him wield the sword."

"And I guess those you go after don't live to tell," he added. "Still, how can they be so dumb? You're his heir."

"I'm his daughter. For that alone, they think me useless. In case you hadn't noticed, the patriarchy thrives under Vampire rule by simple virtue that males are physically stronger. And once they are changed, even more so. It doesn't help that the females who are chosen are often delicate little things."

"You're delicate appearing, but I know for a fact you're strong."

"Because of our bloodline, and it's part of why our enemies tried to get rid of us."

"Your dad never remarried?"

"His heart was too broken after my mother's passing."

"And you're the only thing left of her, making him uber protective."

"I don't know what he'd do if he lost me," she softly agreed.

"Good thing those idiots underestimated you," was his vehement reply. He'd never make that mistake.

She laughed. "Funny how a puppy is the only smart one in our court."

"Cuter too," he added just to hear her snort. Then because he had a masochist side, "So this guy you're negotiating with, you don't love him?" He was pretty sure he knew the answer but wanted confirmation.

"He's likeable enough. Handsome. Mannerly. Can hold an intelligent conversation."

"Sounds boring."

"He is for a vampire."

"What if you get hitched to Mr. Boring and later fall in love?"

"One, I don't believe in love, and two, it will depend on our contract. Monogamy will have to be negotiated, and it won't come cheap."

"I'd never agree to anything else." The mere thought of her with this other dick boiled his blood. Problem being he had no right to jealousy. She'd done everything in her power to make sure he didn't even remember their intimate moments. He was the one foolishly clinging to a dream where she embraced him openly.

"I've heard Lycans are very loyal. And the mated ones supposedly only ever love once," she remarked.

"Don't know. Haven't been around many Lycans."

"Do you wonder what it would have been like had you chosen to join a pack rather than work for my father?"

"Honestly, not much. Packs are tight knit. A little too tight if you ask me. I'm a man who likes his space. It's why working for Lord Augustus is ideal. He keeps me busy with work, and we meet once a month for us to discuss Lycan and Vampire affairs."

"I thought that was just an excuse to drink old brandy and smoke cigars."

He grinned. "That too. Truth is there's not much to

discuss. The Cabal just likes having someone close by keeping an eye."

"So you're spying for them?"

"It might surprise you to hear my loyalty is to Lord Augustus."

"It doesn't. I know he trusts you. Otherwise, we wouldn't be in this car together. Speaking of which, where are we going?"

"To the coast. Wales to be exact."

"Isn't that the site of the only Pack allowed on the island?"

"We won't be going anywhere near them. I've got us a cottage by the cliffs. Not too far from town if we need supplies, but we won't be going out much."

"Planning to keep me locked up for my own good?"

"I'm sure we can find things to do to pass the time." Naked things if he had his way.

They drove, taking turns at the halfway mark because he wasn't about to disparage her driving skills —even if he braced more than once as she raced tight curves.

Each time she laughed, but she also complimented, "Janey handles very well."

"Told you she was a star."

"And is Janey, the woman you named the car after, also the bar set for your lovers?"

"Not anymore."

"Oh, someone knocked her out?" She pretended slight interest, a little too casual.

"Yup."

"And yet you're single. What happened? Did you get cold feet, or did she dump you?"

"More like she keeps putting me in the friend zone."

"You speak as if she's still in your life."

He noticed her tight grip on the wheel. "Since I moved to London, as a matter of fact. She was my first hookup."

The car swerved so violently he smacked off the door. "Everything okay, princess?"

"I need some air."

"Not exactly wise given we're a few hours from dawn."

"We're almost there." She waved at him as she bounced out of the car.

He followed. "You seem agitated."

"Not one bit."

She lied, and he knew it. He could have let her keep believing he'd spoken of another woman. Could have riled her jealousy more. But...he wasn't a dick.

"That friend I was telling you about?"

"The one I couldn't care less about?" she huffed.

"She's kind of above me in status. Not just kind of,

but way over my head. And for ten years she's been pretending we didn't hook up."

She stiffened.

"So I've been pretending too. Pretending that the night we met wasn't epic for me. Pretending that I don't give a shit. Pretending I don't care she's looking to marry another guy. Hoping this road trip we're on will finally change things."

She whirled to face him. "We've never been together."

"Oh yes, we have. Most recently on that ferry. I remember everything, princess. The taste of you. The way you sound when you come. For more than a decade I've been trying to forget. To erase what I feel when I'm around you. But I can't."

"You can't remember because I mesmerized you."

"You tried." He shrugged. "Didn't work."

"Try harder." She appeared really agitated as she paced.

"Actually, I'm done trying to find someone who makes me feel like you do."

"What's that supposed to mean?"

"It means, princess, that I want you, and I'm pretty sure you want me too. Which means your almost-fiancé can find himself another Vampire princess because you are mine."

Her slap seemed to indicate she didn't agree.

8

BROCK REMEMBERED EVERYTHING.

The shock just about had her tearing off his head.

But then he'd be dead, and she didn't want him dead. She also didn't want him realizing she liked him. Juvenile, yes, but she couldn't help it, and that made her grumpy.

"Now, princess, don't be mad."

"I'll be mad if I fucking want to! Why has it taken you ten years to tell me?" she yelled.

"Because, at first, I was kind of peeved. I mean I get it. The lady didn't want it known she slummed with a dog."

"That wasn't the reason."

"Then why?"

"Because."

"That's your answer?"

"Because it's complicated."

"Welcome to life," he grumbled.

"You have to understand that people who get close to me become targets." She'd had a lover who'd been bribed into spying on her, sending copies of her texts with her father to someone in the court. They both died. It proved to be a lesson that she couldn't trust anyone.

"You think I haven't been approached?" He snorted. "Not all of us can be bought."

"But you can be killed. Look at what's happened in the last few days."

He grinned. "A few scratches, a bit of adrenaline fun, and a hot chick. Living the dream, princess."

She gaped. "You almost died."

"Almost being the key word. And now who's acting as if I can't take care of myself? I've survived worse."

"Until you don't. What if they take you hostage to try and manipulate me?"

"One, that would imply you cared, and I'd be good with that. Two, you'd save me, or I'd save myself, and we'd both show them why we shouldn't be messed with."

"You make it sound simple," she grumbled.

"It's not, but at least I'm willing to try."

He said that now, but eventually he'd tire of the shenanigans or die or be corrupted, forcing her to kill him. And that was if he survived her father's wrath if he ever found out a Lycan dared defile his daughter.

"Why would you risk yourself?" she asked.

"Because I think you're worth it." Words to render her silent. "Now get your ass in the car. I want you inside before dawn."

She got back in but sulked, a new thing for her. "Why are you telling me this now? Why wait this long?"

"Given your lack of interest, I didn't want to sound like a fool panting after you. I tried to move on. Forget. But you've ruined me, princess. No one compares."

She knew that feeling. She thought she'd lost her taste for blood. Turned out, she just wanted a specific flavor. "If I'd known, I would have never—"

His turn to grip the steering wheel in agitation. "Don't say it, or I will pull over right now and prove you a liar."

"Excuse me?"

"You have the hots for me. Just like I'm horny as fuck for you. So how about instead of us tiptoeing around it, we stop fighting it."

"Just like that?"

"We'll be in a cottage alone for days, maybe weeks. If ever there was a time to indulge, it's now."

"And what of after?"

"Guess that depends on if we're sick of each other or not."

"So fuck until we get it out of our system?" Her crude question.

"Yes. But you and I both know we have more than just chemistry going for us. We like each other."

"Speak for yourself." A surly lie.

"Come on, princess. For years now you've been dropping into my garage a few times a week."

"To ensure you weren't screwing around with my remodels." It was surprising her father never asked why she kept rebuilding cars. given she didn't drive all that often.

"Why are you so afraid to admit you like me?"

"Because it would complicate things."

"Didn't think you were one to shy away from a challenge."

"I'm not!" She hotly rose to his bait. "But as you mentioned, there are several obstacles should we decide to become a couple in public."

"Then we find a way to make it work."

"Where would we live?" she tossed out. "Because I highly doubt the flock will be accepting of a Lord's heir living openly with a Lycan in the compound." A good portion of the court lived in the massive mansion that sprawled on acres of land right on the edge of London.

"No offense, but I'm too old to be living with

anyone's parents. With the garage gone, it's a good time for me to scout out a new place to work. Something with a basement that we can convert into a master suite."

He countered every argument. "You're serious."

"Yup."

"I'm almost engaged."

"Yeah, we'll see about that," Brock drawled. "I ain't the sharing type."

"You won't have a choice. I need to feed," she pointed out.

"You'll feed on me."

That had her snorting. "One man can't handle it. We rotate donors in between feedings to ensure they aren't too weakened. Which reminds me, if we stay longer than a few days, I'll need to find someone."

"I'm not just any man, princess. I will handle *all* your needs." He offered her a toothy grin, and she sighed.

"You're stubborn."

"And delicious."

Indeed, he was, and damn him for not giving her any way out. At the same time, she didn't want to say no. Men didn't ardently pursue her unless it was to get close to her father. But Brock was already close to her dad. Brock saw her, all of her—bitchy, demanding, fierce, scarred—and he remained attracted.

Maybe he had a point and it was past time they stopped pretending. This place they'd be hiding out would offer them a chance to see if there was something more than just lust. More than just forbidden attraction. Allow her to figure out why she couldn't stay away from this man. Find out if she could trust him.

And if not... He'd said it himself. She wasn't to be underestimated.

"Very well."

"Very well what?" he asked.

"Let's see if you can both feed me and please me."

The car lurched forward, the speed increasing.

"Are we being chased?" She glanced over her shoulder.

"You said yes, which means we are wasting time on the road when we could be in bed fucking."

"Oh." Speechless. Wouldn't her father be surprised? He would also be horrified by her choice. Never mind the fact he enjoyed Brock's company. Sleeping with his daughter? "If my father finds out, he will most likely kill you."

"Ask me if I care. I can't keep living this way, princess. I gotta know."

"Know what?"

He glanced at her as he said, "If you're the one."

She clamped her lips because the very idea...titillated her to the core.

Was this fluttery feeling she got around him love? She wasn't sure. She loved her father, but it wasn't the same, not even close.

Somehow, despite not having a navigation system, Brock knew the roads to take and pulled up outside a cottage with a white picket fence twined with vines set not far from a cliff. The garden had wilted, the approaching winter making the nights too cold. The house itself was what they termed cozy, whitewashed stone walls, a gray slate roof, windows with shutters shut tight. A chimney indicated a fireplace.

He parked the car and exited, heading for the potted plant on the stoop. He rose and waggled a key.

She emerged more slowly, not yet worried about dawn, given they still had more than an hour. She couldn't hear the water, but she smelled it, the cliffs within walking distance. The view must be spectacular. With a full moon in a few days, she'd actually get to enjoy it.

"Why don't you get inside and get comfortable while I get some firewood," he offered, handing over the key.

Their fingers touched. Their gazes met.

He growled. "No tempting me yet. I want you inside, safe from dawn before we start."

"Start what?"

"The most epic sex of your un-life." He winked.

A fluttery response had her lips parting. He went around the side of the cottage, and she unlocked the door. She entered a clean if simple space. It smelled abandoned, a fine layer of dust on the ledges indicating it had been a while since someone had been by. A faint scent of its previous occupant remained.

A scent she knew.

When Brock entered with an armload of wood, she whirled. "This isn't a rental."

"Is this the right time to mention I own the place?"

She arched a brow. "You?"

"Why is that so hard to believe?"

"Because this is a home and not a bachelor pad."

"I plan to retire here one day. Hence why I bought it. When I need to escape the city, I come here."

"What of the Wales Pack?"

"What of them? You do realize it consists of six grizzled old men who like to sit at the bar and reminisce about the old days."

"I got the impression it was larger."

"Maybe in the past, but last time I ran into them about five, six years ago, they'd lost their alpha and were so desperate for a new one, they asked me."

"And you said no?" She couldn't fathom turning down that kind of power.

"Ain't interested in ruling."

"Me either, but with my brother gone..." She shrugged.

"Then let's hope your dad lives forever."

Her lips curved. "The last time I said that to him, he threatened to run away and leave me with his job."

He faked a shudder. "Perish the idea."

Her lips curved. "I'm not eager to inherit the role. Part of why I was looking for a husband. I figured if my father had someone to groom, he'd leave me to my own pursuits."

"To do what?"

She almost didn't say it, only to blurt out, "I miss playing the violin."

"Why did you stop?"

She shrugged. "At first because I mourned. Then because it didn't seem right that I could play when my siblings and mother couldn't."

"So punish yourself for living? That makes a lot of sense."

She grimaced. "I know. It took a while to realize that I wouldn't dishonor them if I chose to enjoy life, but it's been so long."

"Isn't playing an instrument like riding a bike?"

"I hope so," she replied softly. It felt odd to be revealing such an intimate thing, but at the same time, he'd offered her honesty. How could she do any less?

He knelt and threw some logs into the fireplace, getting it going as she wandered around and paid more attention to the little details.

The kitchen was stocked with cans of vegetables and freeze-dried fruits. The fridge was mostly empty except for a container of ice cream in the freezer being over taken by the frost.

He came up behind her, and she didn't flinch or whirl to grab him by the balls and tell him to back off.

"I'll do a grocery run when the stores open. If that's okay?"

"Are you asking me permission?" she turned to ask with incredulity.

"I'll have to leave you alone for about an hour or more. It's twenty minutes to town."

"I'll be fine. I can protect myself."

"It will be daytime."

"How tight are the shutters?"

"Pretty decent, but anyone can open them from the outside."

She glanced around. "Do you have any closets?"

"Actually, I can do one better. I've got a cellar. Mind you, it's not up to your standards, given I wasn't expecting you to ever come here."

"Why not? Weren't you the one who claimed he's been lusting after me for a decade?"

"Never thought you'd ever agree."

A hatch in the floor, hidden under a knotted rag rug, revealed wooden steps going down.

She hesitated.

He clomped down first, pulling a string to light a single bulb over the stairs. Another one illuminated the surprisingly large space. It had been left open except for the support pillars and, unlike most basements, remained mostly uncluttered. Shelves lined the walls, most of them empty.

The most important thing? No windows. Also no secondary exit. She glanced at the hatch.

He read her mind. "Not ideal, I know. But I don't plan to let anyone get close to here. If you're worried about someone coming into the place, I can wait until dark to head into town."

"Stop mollycoddling me."

"I will coddle you if I want. And don't worry, any house I buy will have more than one way in and out. Even if I have to build it myself," he declared before heading up the stairs. She heard some thumping then a hollered, "Move away from the bottom. Incoming."

She shifted to a far corner and watched him heave a mattress down the steps. Once he'd centered it in the middle, he returned upstairs for pillows and bedding. As he leaned down to spread them on the bed, she pounced.

Literally. She tackled him to the mattress and pinned him, easily. He didn't fight at all.

"You know, for a man who declared himself in lust with me, you've yet to—"

He flipped her onto her back and covered her with his body. "I was trying to be a gentleman. It was a long trip. You must be tired. Grimy."

"Horny." She laced her arms around his neck. "So why don't we see if we're as compatible as you think?"

He didn't hesitate at her invitation.

His lips met hers in a passionate kiss that had her tingling. The weight of him atop her was just right. Only their clothes stood in their way. A frenzied need filled them, and their hands tore at fabric, her loose garments easily shed, his ripped in her haste.

Their mouths clung together the entire time, and she panted at the taste of him, the anticipation making her ache.

Once naked, they collapsed to the makeshift bed, skin to skin, him scorching hot to her cool. Tantalizing. Her hands skimmed his flesh, tracing and learning the lines she'd been studying for years. Finally living the fantasy she'd masturbated to so many, many nights.

The heavy weight of him pressed on her, and her legs parted to allow him to settle between.

When his lips moved to caress the shell of her ear, she

huffed impatiently, her fingers digging into his shoulders. He dragged his mouth down her neck, and she shivered. The pressure of his teeth on flesh had her quivering.

But he didn't mark her. She almost begged him to.

Instead, she dragged his head back to a place where they could kiss again, their open mouths allowing tongues to slide and tease. The pleasure from just kissing might have lasted longer, but she'd waited so long. They both had, their small previous interludes just a precursor to this moment.

She wiggled under him, hoping he understood.

"Don't rush me," was his growled reply.

He did stop kissing her, only to slide down enough to grab a puckered nipple with his mouth. He latched on, sucking it, drawing the peak into his mouth, the sensation sending a jolt right down to her sex.

When he used his teeth to graze and bite down gently, she arched and cried out.

He hummed in pleasure against her flesh and shifted sideways, still lavishing attention on her breasts while his hand trailed down her body to cup her mound.

Her breath caught as he used her own lubrication to wet her clit and tease it. He rubbed, and her hips arched, wanting more.

"Taste me," she begged.

"My pleasure," he rumbled in reply. He slid down

to between her legs, pushing her thighs farther apart that he might lick her. He toyed with her clit, sliding his tongue back and forth over it. But when he thrust his fingers into her sex, she started bucking, her body tight with need.

He held her down as she thrashed, his mouth pleasuring her sensitized flesh. Her tension coiled as her orgasm neared. He knew it and didn't stop. He kept playing with her until a wave hit, bowing her body, stopping her breath.

The orgasm rolled through her and kept going as he continued to lap and tease, bringing back that tension.

She panted and clawed at him. "Brock."

"I've got you, princess." He rose to cover her body. The thick head of his cock nudged the pulsing entrance to her sex.

He kissed her, the taste of her still on his lips. She moaned and opened her eyes to see him already watching her as he sank into her, stretching and filling her.

Together they found a rhythm, thrusting in and out, the length of him enough to find her inner sweet spot. Over and over. She tried to keep her eyes open, but the pleasure had her throwing her head back, her body tight with need. He pounded into her harder.

She growled. "More."

He gave it to her. A piston that had her keening as an orgasm ripped through her. In her frenzy, she sank her teeth into his shoulder.

The succulent taste of his blood kept her climax going and drew his own pleasure. He bucked and even howled as her sex milked him, dragging him into an extended orgasm that left them both sated.

The first man to not only blow her mind sexually but she'd never felt so satisfied eating from anyone else. Was it any wonder she began to drowse as the sun came up.

She smiled as he kissed her bare shoulder before covering it. He shut the hatch, but even so, she heard the purr of the car as he left.

What did it mean that she couldn't wait until he came back?

9

THE MOMENT BROCK left the bed with the slumbering—and slightly smiling Arianna—he wanted to turn around and go right back. However, this was his best moment to get supplies before an enemy tracked them down. Once he'd done an initial grocery run, he could arrange to have deliveries to keep them going. Or to prevent leading someone to his cottage, he could take Arianna with him to shops that stayed open later. It would just require a little more driving. Small towns were great, but many chose a more nine-to-five approach, especially in the off-season.

He raced into town, or at least tried to. A tractor on the road slowed him right down. Then the store had only one clerk for checkout. To top things off, as he walked out, he ran into Elmer, one of the Lycans in the Wales Cliff Pack.

EVE LANGLAIS

Elmer's eyes widened at the sight of Brock. "What are you doing here?"

The surprise in his tone had Brock eyeing the other man. A man who didn't smell the same as before. Still Lycan, but with an undertone that bothered.

"Hey, Elmer. Just taking a holiday by the sea. How have you and the others been?" he asked politely. The last time he'd seen Elmer was a year ago. He'd been almost begged Brock to take over management of the pack. Once their alpha died, they'd been unable to attract a new one due to the restriction the Vampires placed on Lycans living on the island. Essentially, no more than a dozen were allowed, and each new recruit had to swear fealty to Lord Augustus.

"I'm f-fine," the man stammered.

Brock arched a brow. "You seem awfully nervous. Is there something wrong?" While he'd turned down the alpha offer, Brock did remain a liaison of sorts between the Vampires and Lycans.

"Just shocked to see you around given you're famous and all. I hear the cops are looking for you for questioning." The man seemed bolstered by the reminder that Brock was a wanted man.

"It's a good thing you're not the type to snitch."

That had Elmer drawing himself straight. "Of course I wouldn't."

"Then I don't see a problem." But Brock was now

glad he'd told no one of this home. The times he'd visited, he'd always let the Wales Cliff Pack think he was staying at a nearby hotel or B&B. "Did you ever find a solution to your alpha problem?"

The reply came with eyes slewing left. "Nope."

Brock could have let it go, but he leaned forward. "Why are you lying to me?"

The accusation brought a tremble to Elmer's hands, and he blubbered, "You shouldn't be here. It's not safe."

"I'm aware. Wanted man and all."

"Not safe for any Lycans, especially an alpha," Elmer insisted.

"What's going on?"

Elmer opened his mouth just as someone shouted, "Hey, old man, you going to stop yapping and get the ale we came for?"

A glance to an older, beaten-up Volkswagen showed an unkempt man Brock didn't recognize, having a cigarette in the car. Talk about mistreating a classic.

"Friend of yours?" he drawled.

"I gotta go. You should leave too." Elmer practically ran inside, and Brock walked his groceries past Janey and around the corner. He set them down and waited.

Sure enough, Scruffy Dude soon poked his nose

around the corner, and Brock snagged him in a headlock.

"Looking for something?" he growled.

The man stiffened. "Who are you?"

"Funny, I was going to ask you the same thing."

"Let me go." The scruffy guy struggled, and Brock waited until the fellow realized he couldn't get loose.

"Ready to talk now? Name."

"Kevin." A sullen reply.

"See how easy that was, Kevin? Now, let's try another easy question. Who's the new alpha for the Pack?"

"Don't know what you're talking about."

He squeezed enough the man tapped his arm, unable to breathe. When he eased the pressure, Kevin blabbed, "I don't know nothing about no alpha."

Kevin didn't appear to lie, and yet Brock's nose insisted he held a Lycan. "And yet you're obviously part of the Pack since you're hanging with Elmer. Did he bite you?"

"Fuck no. I don't swing that way."

Brock got more confused. "How did you become Lycan?" A direct question.

"As if you don't know. You're one of us."

Us, implying there were more. "I asked you how." He squeezed, and the guy grabbed at his arm as if he could pry it off. He couldn't. When the guy went limp, close to passing out, Brock eased up again.

"Well?"

"Blood transfusion. Only took me three sessions," Kevin boasted.

The claim made his blood run cold. "You weren't bitten?"

"Fuck no," the guy huffed.

"Who gave you the blood?"

"Fuck you. I ain't telling you shit."

"Oh really?" Brock once more choked him out enough to have the guy begging.

Only this time Kevin remained belligerent. "Beat me. I don't care. I heal fast now. Just wait until I tell them about you."

"Tell who?"

"You'll soon see. You messed with the wrong bloke. We own this town, this coast. And we're getting bigger all the time. Meaning there's nowhere you can hide from us." The man snickered as he pulled a knife. "But you won't be running. You're gonna come with me unless you want to bleed."

Threats? Oh hell no. For one, this little fucker was obviously an aberration because Lord Augustus hadn't heard of any new Lycans, meaning the Wales Pack broke the treaty. Two, his claims indicated a new alpha was not only using a different method of Lycan-making but also creating more than allowed. Something Brock highly doubted the Cabal had approved. And finally, Brock didn't like his attitude, his smell, or the danger this fucker posed not only to him but to Arianna. It left him only one real choice to ensure the asshole never tattled.

Cold? More like reality. Lycans couldn't afford to be soft.

The alley behind the store wasn't London with its many cameras or a busy spot with druggies shooting up and prostitutes plying their wares. It was an empty loading area with a handy dumpster.

Brock didn't give Kevin a chance for final words. Or begging. With a sharp twist, he snapped his neck and put the garbage out. Once he'd covered him in the dumpster and shut the lid, he grabbed his groceries and kept an eye out before heading to his car. No one was in the parking lot. Elmer hadn't yet returned with his purchase of ale.

He waited for the older man to return, leaning against the abused Volkswagen, spattered in mud so thick the license plate wasn't readable. Only Elmer never exited the store, and when Brock returned inside to check, he could find no sign of him.

Fuck.

For a second, he thought about hunting the guy down, but he'd already been gone too long. He could only hope Elmer did the smart thing and kept his mouth shut.

He took a circuitous route to the cottage, glad he'd never placed it in his real name but rather that of the corporation he'd created to hide the bulk of the money he'd made restoring cars. A man who might have to disappear always had a backup plan. Only he didn't want to flee. Not yet.

Something had happened to the Wales Cliff Pack. Blood transfusions instead of a bite? It made him think of his conversation with Gunner. How some mad scientist was experimenting and creating wolfmen. He put in a call, but Gunner didn't answer, so Brock left a message. "Call me." To the point.

No one appeared to be following him, and so he made his way to the cottage. Once he put the groceries away, he set about protecting the place. Trip wires in the garden. Bells on the gate. He even lugged out the box of mouse traps and set them out at random. Anything to give them notice.

He wouldn't run with Arianna, not yet. Only Elmer knew he was in the area, and Elmer looked scared. Whether more scared of Brock or the people running his pack remained to be seen.

Agitated, he called Gunner again. He answered on the second ring. "You know, I didn't call you the other day so we could become phone buddies," his old mate complained.

Rather than fuck around with niceties, Brock went straight to the point. "That crazy doc you were dealing with in Romania, how was he making those wolf dudes?"

"Why?" was the cagey reply.

"I might have a situation." He explained the odd conversation.

Gunner paused before saying, "Could be he was fucking with you."

"Maybe, but I can't help thinking about the monsters we were dealing with in the city."

"I thought those things were hybrids of a few animals."

"But they did have some wolf," he insisted.

"And bat, according to Silver. Which coincidentally is related to Vampires."

He snorted. "I can assure you they don't change into bats. That's a myth."

"Good to know. As for how Sascha was doing it... Don't know. His lab got blown up."

"But you said he escaped."

"He did.

"And didn't you say he often visited the UK?" Brock further questioned.

"Supposedly visiting an elderly aunt."

"Meaning he could have fled here."

"Yup. And before you ask, I don't have an address for this aunt, but I can dig around and see if anyone in the village knows anything."

"Do you have a picture of this Sascha?"

"I can gather a few and send them to you. He's kind of obvious, given he's got a chin to forehead scar. But let me add, you should not go after him yourself. If he's been playing monster god in Wales, then chances are he's got a mini army."

"An army that's been attacking m—" He almost said my mate, but changed it to, "me and others."

"Where are you?"

He hesitated.

"Don't tell me you don't trust me?" Gunner exclaimed.

"I trust you, but I gotta be careful." A hasty reassurance. "Should we call in the Cabal for reinforcements?"

"I wouldn't. I told you the Cabal is compromised," Gunner stated.

"Well, I should inform Lord Augustus at the very least."

"Do me a favor and hold off telling anyone."

"Why?"

"Because if Sascha is in Wales, we can't have him tipped off."

"Augustus wouldn't tattle."

"Maybe not, but if he musters his flock, can you say the same for them?"

He sighed. "Fuck me. What are we going to do?"

"Nothing until I get there."

"Nothing? Seriously?"

"Fine, learn to needlepoint, do a puzzle, catch up on Netflix, but stay away from town and people until you've got some backup."

"Why, Gunner, you almost sound like you care."

"Fuck off, asshole. And try to not die until I get there."

They hung up, and he went back inside then down into the basement to find Arianna still sleeping.

He spent that time checking news reports out of Wales. Missing people. Animal attacks. Both of which there appeared to be more of than usual, especially in the last year.

Late afternoon, he got a text from the princess. An emoji actually.

A peach. An eggplant. And a winkie face.

Despite the situation, he flew down those steps into the arms of his Vampire princess.

Only after she was sated, both with blood and an epic orgasm, did he say, "We might have a problem."

10

Brock's dire announcement of a problem didn't ruin her after-sex-and-feeding glow, but Arianna rolled onto her side to face him.

"Explain," she demanded.

"Short version, someone's taken over the Wales Cliff Pack."

Her brow furrowed. "How is that an issue? Weren't they in need of an alpha?"

"Yes, but it doesn't appear as if that's what they got. I ran into Elmer at the market." He told her everything that happened while she slept, including his conversation with his old army buddy, Gunner.

At the end, she summarized. "So let me get this straight, a mad scientist doing experiments with Lycan genetics and creating wolfmen might have fled

Romania to the UK and resumed his dabbling using the Wales Pack."

"Yes."

Her brain kept processing and arrived at the most logical conclusion. "Meaning he's most likely behind our monster issues in London."

"Possibly."

She arched a brow. "It would be a huge coincidence if he weren't."

"The monsters we encountered weren't wolfmen. Not entirely," he hastened to add.

"Do you really think there are many mad scientists running around capable of doing such a thing?"

"When you put it that way..." he grumbled. "We can ask Gunner about it when he gets here."

"Ah yes, the friend who thinks we should hide so he can arrive and rescue us."

"More or less." Brock offered a sheepish shrug.

"You do realize that's not going to happen," she offered rather tartly.

He grinned. "Why do you think I told you? Between the two of us, at the very least, we can locate the pack and figure out what's going on. If it's too much for us to handle, then we wait for Gunner, maybe even involve your father."

Her turn to make a face. "Only as a last resort." Daddy dear had sent her away to get her out of harm's way. He wouldn't be happy to hear she went looking for it.

"Before we start hunting, promise you won't do anything rash."

"Who me?" She offered a sweet smile.

He groaned. "Your father is going to murder me if anything happens to you."

"Only if I die, so don't let that happen."

"Trust me, the last thing I want, princess, is for this to end." He drew her close for a kiss.

A kiss she enjoyed too much. Giving in hadn't curbed her craving for him yet. Not even close. Which might be why she mounted him for another round. Might as well. The sun hadn't yet set.

She didn't bite him when she came. She remained riding him, hips rotating as his hands gripped her breasts, teasing her nipples.

Once the climax receded, she rose and stretched. "Now that's how I like waking up." And to think she'd denied herself this pleasure for more than a decade.

"I could get used to this," he agreed.

She didn't point out the hurdle to them being together once they returned to London. The ban on their kind associating still existed. Even if it didn't, she remained very aware of his mortal life span versus hers. As it stood, she was more than a decade older than him even if her appearance said otherwise.

"I'm hungry," she announced.

He grinned at her from their bed on the basement floor. "Feel free to have me as a snack."

"For actual food. And you should have some, too, if you're going to keep up with me."

"Don't worry about me, princess." He rose, lean tempting muscles making her rethink her hunger.

"I will worry, because you're the one who insists I feed exclusively from you, which requires you keeping up your strength. Our donors are on a very special diet, high in iron and other nutrients."

"Good thing I bought us some steaks and a spinach salad for dinner then."

"I thought you couldn't cook."

"Pre-seasoned meat that just requires singeing on both sides on the barbecue, and the salad is premade. Just add a dressing and toss."

"Sounds delicious." She headed for the stairs.

"Sun's not down yet."

"Are the shutters closed?"

"Yeah."

"I'll be fine. I want to shower and dress before we head out."

His eyes widened. "Shit, I completely forgot to get you clothes when in town. The Elmer and Kevin thing threw me for a loop."

Her lips pursed. "Then I guess we'll be shopping first before hunting."

"Not many choices for that after dark. I have a better idea." He eyed her up and down. "You're about the same size."

"Same size as who?" she asked slowly.

He grinned. "You'll see. Think you'll be okay for fifteen or so minutes?"

She reached for her scabbard with its sword. "Anyone interrupts my shower, and I won't need dinner."

He dragged her close for a kiss. "You're sexy when you're violent."

"You're not too bad yourself, for a dog," she added then laughed as he slapped her ass going up the stairs.

The shutters did a good job of blocking daylight. The little that filtered in wasn't enough to bother her skin.

"Lock the door behind me, and if you hear anything, take cover," he cautioned as he headed out.

His overprotectiveness annoyed. *I'm capable of defending myself.* At the same time, it was nice to be treated as if she were worth protecting.

The water pressure in his shower left much to be desired, as did the very bland soap. By the time she emerged refreshed, Brock had returned and was spreading various articles of clothing over the sofa.

She neared him and grimaced. "Smells like moth balls."

"The cottage up the road is closed for the season, but the owners like to travel light. The wife is close to your size."

She held up a pink sweatshirt with two fingers. "Do I look like a person who wears pastels?"

"I prefer you wearing nothing. However, that might cause a stir if we're going hunting."

"As if I wouldn't be noticed dressed like a giant bonbon."

"Well, you are sweet and tasty."

"No." She tossed it aside.

"Then how about this?" He held up a darker sweater.

In the end, she managed an outfit that would have gotten her mocked by the flock. The pants were a few inches short and ended above her ankles. The gray T-shirt was loose around her chest, as was the navy knit sweater she layered over it. At least she still had her boots.

She dug through the pile of garments, and Brock asked, "What are you looking for?"

"If I say something to act as a mask, are you going to be annoying about it?"

"Yes, because you shouldn't hide your face. You're beautiful."

"Yeah. Yeah. Maybe to you, but anyone else who sees me is going to point and be like look at the lady with the giant scar, which will lead to attention, and I thought we were avoiding that."

He pursed his lips. "People are assholes."

"Agreed." She held up a solid-colored T-shirt in green. Horrendous. She ripped it.

"Wait. If you must, I've got a better option." He went digging in his kitchen cupboards, then outside before returning, waving his find with a triumphant smile. "Look what I found in my glove box. Left over from the pandemic."

The black paper surgical mask felt stifling after the last few days without one. But she wasn't about to admit it to Brock. He'd tell her to take it off.

And she just might.

But the reality was people would be more likely to notice and remember the woman with the scar on her face and not the lady in a mask. Even now, years after the pandemic, people still sometimes wore them in public so she wouldn't be completely out of place.

"Ready?" she asked.

"We don't even know where we're going," he remarked. "Or are we just going to drive around randomly and hope we find an arrow that says bad guys this way."

"Does the Wales Pack not have a den they meet in?"

He shook his head. "There was never more than a dozen, so when they had a pack gathering, it was usually at the alpha's house. But we don't know who their new leader is."

"According to you, the guy you killed arrived in a car and his companion left without it. If it's still in the parking lot, then we might find a clue."

"Okay, but we might have to wait to check it out, given it's just after dinner and people will still be around. I'd rather not draw attention."

She eyeballed him. "Ah yes, that reminds me, you're a wanted man. There's a chance pedestrians we encounter will have seen your image on the news."

"The picture shows me with a full beard." He rubbed his bristled jaw.

"You were recognized just this morning."

"Only because of my scent."

"We'll tackle that in a moment. Do you have another of these?" She pointed to the mask.

"Why? Do you need a second?"

"Not for me. You."

He grimaced. "Don't make me wear one. I hate them."

"Suck it up, puppy. We can be the neurotic couple.

No one will give us a second glance, especially once we douse ourselves in cologne."

"I don't have cologne."

"Then I guess we'll have to improvise."

He practically gagged by the time she finished. The kitchen spray cleaner left his hands and the jacket she also spritzed with a lemony scent. She stuck with her mothball perfume.

They left the cottage, and he grumbled as he drove them to town. "Gonna smell us from a mile away."

"And not know who's coming, which is perfect."

"You're a smartass, princess."

"I know." Her reply was smug.

The town was cute. Quaint. And all the other things touristy brochures loved to take pictures of. Despite being a city girl, she rather liked it. None of the buildings more than a few stories, each of them unique.

They parked a few blocks from the grocery store and wandered, hand in hand. Few people were out given dark came early and the evenings had grown chilly. A few restaurants and taverns showed signs of life, with patrons eating and drinking. The homes had their drapes drawn, with the flicker of televisions showing people settled in for the night.

As they passed the grocery store, she noticed the lone car parked.

"That's it," he muttered.

"Let's go around to the back first. I want to see the body."

"Why?"

"Did you check his pockets for an ID?" she asked.

"No. At the time, I was more concerned with getting rid of it."

"Here's to hoping it hasn't been found."

He led her to the place in the alley with the dumpster, only to exclaim, "It's gone!"

"But no crime scene tape," she murmured.

"Looks more like the garbage got taken given the whole thing is empty. I wonder how long until they notice they found a body."

"If they crushed it with the garbage? Most likely never," she opined. "Grocery stores throw out a lot of stuff, including meat." Which drew predators like feral vamps—the ones that didn't take properly. A tiny tidbit that she knew because those kinds of aberrations required extermination before they caused havoc among the human population. The only safe Vampires were the hidden ones.

"Fuck me, I wish I'd though to frisk him before dumping his ass." His lips turned down.

"Not all is lost," she reminded. "Let's check out the car."

"If it's unlocked," he added.

She snorted. "As if that will stop me."

They emerged into the parking lot and saw no one around, but still, she had a plan. She grabbed Brock's hand and dragged him close for a kiss.

"I thought we were supposed to be searching the car," he murmured against her lips.

"We are. But if anyone is watching, we shouldn't look obvious about it." She pushed away from him and walked far enough that when she dragged him in for another kiss, she could lean against the vehicle. It proved distracting to have his hot lips on hers while she groped for the handle. The passenger side door opened.

"Shall we?" she purred, shoving him onto the seat so he sat with his legs outside the car. She then crouched between his spread knees.

He gasped. "I can't believe I'm saying this, but I don't think this is the right time for a blowjob."

She winked at him. "As if you'd tell me to stop if I started."

"Uh..." A glazed reply.

She laughed. "Maybe later. This is cover. Anyone watching will think you're getting head, but in reality, you'll be digging in that glovebox to see if you can find the registration."

"Oh." Definite disappointment in that one syllable.

She put her face against his jean-covered groin and blew. "Later, my big, growly puppy. If you're good."

"Killing me, princess," he complained as he reached into the glove box for a rummage. "Ew."

"What?"

"Exploded ketchup packet. Nasty." He pulled his sticky fingers out.

"Keep looking," she whispered as she did her best to not give in to temptation. She'd not yet put her mouth on him. Now she wondered what he'd taste like. If he'd buck against her lips.

He dug around some more. "Nothing."

She glanced into the footwell covered in chunks of dried mud and saw a receipt. Snared it and read off the address of the gas station.

"Do you know it?" she asked.

"Yeah, it's like the only Texaco in the area."

"Well, that's useless." She pushed away from him, and he exited the car, shutting the door, before saying, "Now what?"

She nibbled the tip of her thumb. "I don't know. You're sure the Wales Pack didn't have a hang-out spot? A bar they liked, maybe?"

He shook his head. "Not that they ever told me."

"What about that guy who recognized you? Do you know where he lives?"

"Yeah. He lives above a bakery a few miles from here."

As she passed the rear of the car, the mud on it caught her eye. "It's dirty," she observed. As in caked with mud. Tires, bottom of the door panels, up in the wheel wells, even the registration plate.

"That didn't happen in town."

"Obviously," she grumbled.

"Did you think this would be easy, princess?"

"I'd hoped we'd get at least a general direction."

"Let's see if Elmer's got anything hiding at his place. Although not sure how we're getting inside."

"Leave that to me."

"Don't tell me your skills run into lock-picking?"

She winked as she said, "You ain't seen nothing yet, puppy."

129

11

Arianna constantly surprised Brock. Take how they'd gone from throwing barbs and innuendos to throwing sexual challenges and promises.

Her claim she'd blow him later almost had him saying fuck the hunt and dragging her back to the cottage. However, duty before pleasure. That duty being to track down the Wales Cliff Pack.

The car had been a bust. The body was gone and hopefully never recovered. As they took Janey a few miles away and parked once more, Arianna did an internet search on the local news. So far, no report on a dead body.

The bakery he led her to was closed for the night and its window dark. The door with the number 34B was unlocked and the flight of stairs to the second story steep. The scent leading them to the top was definitely

Elmer's, but with that new twist, which she remarked on.

"There's something off about his smell," she remarked, her eyes turning dark as she tilted her head back for a deeper breath.

"Well, he definitely wasn't any hairier than usual."

"But possibly tampered with," she noted.

"Yeah." He knocked at the door, even as he didn't expect a reply. A lack of any other personal scent indicated the man resided alone.

"No one's there," she observed. "And before you ask if I am sure, I'm a vampire. We detect heartbeats."

"Even through doors?"

"I can."

Meaning not all of them could. Not surprising in her case. When it came to Vampires, not all of them were created equally.

The doorknob didn't yield to a jiggle. It also wasn't very sturdy.

"Stand back. I'm going to bust it open."

"I do love it when you get physical," she teased as she stood aside.

A shoulder to the door and the frame splintered. A second slam burst it open, and he stepped into the apartment. A quick glance around showed it empty as predicted. "Clear. Come on in."

Arianna stepped inside and grimaced. He could

see why. Elmer lived as a quintessential bachelor, his pad replete with dirty dishes, empty food containers, and bottles strewn all over. It reeked of moldy food, dust, and body odor.

She wrinkled her nose. "Why must be people be so gross? Is it that hard to put things in the trash?"

"Not everyone has a maid," he retorted even as he agreed.

"You don't, and yet you don't live like a pig."

"What can I say? I had enough of maggots and mold when in the army." Just the sight of anything wiggling churned his stomach and made him flash back to his time in the cell when he had a choice of either eating the maggoty food or starving.

"Hard to imagine you as a soldier," she remarked, stepping gingerly among the trash.

"For a guy with no money and no prospects and with okay grades, it was the only real option if I wanted a career."

"Do you miss it?" she asked, her foot nudging a pizza box cautiously as if it might contain a snake.

"Nope. While I do enjoy the company of the men I became friends with, I'm not a guy who likes to be social twenty-four-seven. In the army, especially in the field, you're on top of each of other, in each other's faces constantly."

She shuddered. "Ugh."

"She says despite living in a mega-mansion full of people."

"That I barely talk to," she tartly replied. "I've been thinking of asking my father about renovating the carriage house on the property so I can move out and avoid them."

"That old place overgrown with ivy?" He'd seen it on his visits to Lord Augustus.

"Yes. The second floor is very spacious."

"What are you going to do with the main floor?"

She shrugged. "I don't know. Given its large open space, maybe a gym?"

"Pretty big gym."

"I'm sure I'll think of something."

He wanted to say it would make a great garage, but that might be moving too fast. He walked farther into Elmer's place and thought about putting the mask in his pocket back on his face. "There has to be something wrong with Elmer because I can't see how a Lycan can stand this smell." Not to mention, the last time he'd been here—at Elmer's insistence as he tried to convince Brock to take on the alpha role—while not super clean, it had been tidy.

"What would be the point in experimenting on someone who is already Lycan?" she asked.

"Can one really know what a sick mind is thinking?" he countered.

EVE LANGLAIS

"A wolfman would have its uses, I suppose."

"Such as?" Because he didn't see it. Running on four legs? Way faster than two. Not to mention, while people might be a little freaked at seeing a wolf, they'd lose their ever-loving shit seeing a wolfman.

"Hands to grip weapons or manipulate objects, say like a lock or even a doorknob."

He frowned. That would be handy. "I guess, but I have to wonder about their minds. The monsters we encountered were literal beasts, whereas a shifted Lycan usually still has his wits."

At that claim, she arched a brow. "Going to tell me you never got an urge to snack on people or hunt them?"

"Yes, but I'm still in control."

"But is that true for all Lycan?"

He pressed his lips tight because he couldn't actually answer that. He'd never thought to talk about it with his friends. After all, how would that conversation go? *Hey, you guys ever think of letting loose and tearing out someone's throat for a snack?*

"We should get to searching before someone notices we're here," he suggested.

"Given the state of his living room and kitchen, I think I'll let you tackle the bedroom and bathroom. I cringe to think what nasty surprises lurk in there."

"Gee, thanks. What are we looking for anyhow?

134

Because I highly doubt he's got an address or a map labelled 'mad scientist's lair.'"

"No, but perhaps he's got an address scribbled down for a pack member or perhaps more receipts."

Brock marched into the bedroom, which wasn't as bad as expected. The space reeked of sweat, the sheets grimy from not being washed, the drawers in the dresser pulled out and empty, a few clothing items littered the floor. He nudged them around but found nothing. The closet was mostly empty hangers. The bathroom proved a bust as well, although he did find the unopened deodorant in the cupboard ironic. It occurred to him that there were some basics missing. Where were the rest of Elmer's clothes? His toothbrush and toothpaste? He could see a ring on the edge of the tub where a shampoo bottle used to sit.

When he emerged, she asked, "Find anything?"

"Looks like Elmer skipped town. Either he tossed out most of his clothes and toiletries or he packed his shit and left."

"Seeing you must have spooked him."

"More likely knowing what I did to his buddy, he thought it best to split."

She grinned. "How does it feel to be the big bad wolf he's scared of?"

"If I'd known he was going to run, I would have

pressed him harder." He glanced around. "Did you find anything?"

"No." Her lower lip jutted adorably. Although he would never say it to her face. She was pretty quick with a blade.

"Guess we're pooch out of luck."

Her lips pursed. "Giving up already? What of the other pack members? Do you know where they live?"

"Nah. Elmer was the only one who ever invited me over once the alpha was gone."

"I know my father used you to keep tabs on them. Surely you have some contact info?"

"Not addresses," he said with a shake of his head. "I mean I've got a few phone numbers in my contacts that I could probably call, but then people would know I was looking."

She sighed. "That won't do. We need the element of surprise if we're going to catch this scientist."

"Assuming he's here," he interjected. "We don't have any confirmation."

"You and your details," she grumbled.

"I like to think of it more as not going off half-cocked."

"I forgot you're Mr. Likes-to-be-Prepared," she taunted.

"Having a backup plan isn't a bad thing."

"You should try being more spontaneous."

"Says the woman who tried to make me forget the time we did let loose."

She pursed her lips. "I had my reasons."

"Guess we both have our quirks. Where to next?" His first impulse was to suggest the cottage because it had been hours since he'd last touched her. The craving for her hadn't diminished at all. And he had a feeling it never would. He had ten years of fantasizing to catch up on. Ten years of being close to this mate and being unable to do anything about it. Ten years of trying to deny fate.

No more.

"We must have missed something. Maybe we should check out that car again. We didn't look in the trunk or under the seats."

"Do you really think we'll find anything?"

Her lips turned down. "No."

"You know, I do have a friend who can look up the license plate."

Her expression brightened. "Why didn't you say that before?"

"Because his services ain't cheap."

"Money isn't an object." She waved a hand. "Let's go get it and see if he can get us an address."

"Wow, sexist much, princess? My hacker friend is a she."

"Oh really?" Her tone dropped low and menacing.

EVE LANGLAIS

"Put away those jealous fangs. She's not only old enough to be my mom, she's into chicks, not dicks."

"I am not jealous," she huffed.

"Sure you aren't," he cajoled.

"Let's go." As she headed for the exit, she pointed to the muddy galoshes by the door. "More muck. Interesting."

"Actually, it is." He crouched for a closer look at the dirt. "It's fresh." It squished rather than crumbled when poked.

"Why and where would they be traipsing around getting mud on themselves and a car?"

"There are all kinds of places they could be getting dirty. Wales is huge on farming."

"I doubt they were tilling the land."

Him too. The mud could have come from anywhere.

They exited and got back into Janey. The trip back to the grocery store parking lot didn't take long.

And proved to be useless, because the moment they neared, she exclaimed, "The car is gone!"

12

Arianna could kick herself for not scrubbing the mud to read the license plate earlier. Blame her addled wits for not thinking of running it herself. Brock wasn't the only one with a hacker friend.

Which reminded her of his accusation of jealousy. Accurate. She'd seen red the moment he mentioned the hacker's sex. The stranger thing? She'd never had a green-eyed fit before for any man. Had she been envious of a nice outfit or a sexy car? Yes. But a guy? It disturbed her to realize what it meant.

She'd agreed to become his lover mostly to stop her insane attraction to him. By having the forbidden fruit, she should be able to assuage her desire and cast him aside when she tired of him.

What if that never happened?

A Vampire and a Lycan together as a couple? It

139

broke the rules. It would see her cast aside because her father would have no choice, given the backlash that would occur if it were found out.

They'd have to split up, which bothered her immensely. Meaning they needed more sex and blood. Maybe then he'd start to properly annoy her and she'd have no trouble tearing out his throat. Okay, that was extreme. She'd try dumping him first.

"Earth to Princess. Come in, Princess." He waved a hand in front of her face, and she eyed him.

"I was thinking."

"Yeah, I know, I could see the smoke. What had your mind buzzing?"

She couldn't exactly reveal what she'd been pondering, so instead she latched onto the current situation. "Mud."

"Ah yes, mud, fascinating stuff. Sticks to everything."

"Don't be annoying. It's a clue."

"To the fact Elmer and his buddy didn't like using a car wash?"

"Use your head for something other than a hat rack, puppy. If this mad doctor is in the area conducting experiments, he would require a location where he could work that wouldn't be overrun with nosy neighbors. At the same time, it has to be accessible, as I imagine he requires medical equipment that is sizeable and can't just be carried in."

"Which means not in the village but close by. A holiday cottage perhaps? A rental house?"

"Those would have landlords who might notice a lot of coming and going, not to mention the extra cost of electricity if using medical machinery. By the sounds of it, this doctor might have been at it for months, maybe longer."

"He could have bought a home."

"A distinct possibility, but that would leave a paper trail. Didn't your friend claim he'd taken over an abandoned castle in Romania? Maybe he did the same here."

Brock tapped the steering wheel as he mused aloud. "Somewhere remote, but with a road going in, close enough to town to keep supplied but, at the same time, out of sight. A place with no nosy looky-loos."

"Does that make you think of a location?"

"There are a few abandoned places that might serve as a base of operation."

"Such as?"

"There's a couple of houses that I looked at buying and restoring."

"Any of them with a muddy drive?"

He frowned. "I don't recall. Maybe."

"What about an abandoned castle? You usually can't go far without stumbling across a ruin."

The mention brightened his expression. "Actually, we're not that far from one, the Baron Hills Mansion. Not quite a castle, but definitely a muddy trek to reach, given it was abandoned a while ago. However, I can't see it being a great base of operation given it's just walls and no roof."

"Not that hard to stretch a tarp."

"It wouldn't have any electricity, though."

"Generators are easy to find. Is it remote?"

"Yes, enough that no one would hear anything."

"Meaning we should check it out."

He glanced at her. "Are you sure? It's getting late."

She snorted. "It's not even midnight yet. The night has barely begun."

"Okay, princess, but if we find something, no rushing in. We retreat, report, and wait for reinforcements."

"Spoilsport," she muttered.

"More like a guy who'd like to live to see the dawn, preferably naked with you."

"If I ever see the dawn, I'll die."

"You know what I mean," he snapped.

"I do. And I have every intention of being alive tomorrow and the next day," was her pert reply.

"Good to know."

"I also plan to have sex with you numerous times."

"Trying to wear me out?"

"Something of the sort."

He glanced at her. "And what if we don't tire of each other?"

"We will."

"And let's say it doesn't happen, then what?"

She couldn't look at him as she mumbled, "I don't know."

"Why, princess, are you ashamed of being my lover?"

"No. Yes. It's complicated."

"This supposed rule banning our association is archaic."

"Says the guy led by a Cabal with rules just as regressive and patriarchal."

"Because only men can become Lycans."

"Not true. The Cabal made it illegal to have daughters because they were scared of them," she pointed out. "Hence why Quinn and his little doctor girlfriend are on the run."

"Fine. We're both being hamstrung by stupid laws that need updating. Maybe you and I should be the trendsetters that start the change."

"My father would disown me."

"Don't be so sure of that. Your father loves you."

He did, but would he love her enough to buck tradition and face ostracization by the flocks?

"How far to this ruined mansion?" she asked.

"A good twenty minutes or so, why?"

Rather than reply, she leaned over and unzipped his pants.

"Um, princess, is that a good idea?"

"I need to do something to relax," she murmured, pulling his semi-hard cock free.

"I'd like to not crash us."

"Then pay attention."

"I am. Oh, fuck me." He groaned as she took him into her mouth.

He filled it perfectly, a long, thick shaft covered in velvety skin. The harder it got, the more it pulsed with delicious blood. It was all she could do to contain herself as she bobbed her head, savoring the size of him, the salty taste as he pearled.

He groaned, and she noticed he'd pulled over, too distracted to drive.

It was titillating as hell. She kept dragging her lips up and down his shaft, sucking until her cheeks hollowed. She grazed him with her fangs, and he shuddered.

But it was when he whispered, "Bite me," that she almost lost control.

She'd never drunk while giving head. Then again,

she rarely gave head. She worked him faster, and he panted. His fingers cupped her head. She scratched him with a tooth, enough to make him bleed.

Oh my. She moaned as she savored him, sucked and sucked and his hips jerked, and he thrust into her mouth. She took everything he had to give: his passion, his seed, his blood.

And when it was all over, she knew the answer to his earlier question. Would she be willing to walk away from the flock to be with him?

Yes.

But would that choice destroy them in the end?

When she finally lifted her head, he wore a glazed look on his face as he murmured, "You are so fucking perfect."

"And you apparently can't drive when getting a blowjob."

"Excuse me for losing all sense of control when you touch me, princess," he drawled as they got back onto the road.

"You're excused," she impishly replied with a hint of smug.

His hand came to rest heavily on her thigh and inched up it. It might have even gotten interesting had he not growled, "I see lights coming out of the road going into the manor."

They both forgot about sex as they slumped in

their seats as they drove by the muddy track leading into the woods.

In the mirror, she could see a car emerge and turn the opposite way. They kept going for a bit before he pulled over.

He gave her a glance. "Looks like someone is using the old mansion. But no guarantee it's the scientist."

"Let's go check it out."

He sighed. "I knew you were going to say that."

"Afraid of a little mud, puppy?"

"You kidding? I can't wait until you have to bathe me later," he said with a wink as he got out of the car.

"Guess I'll be scraping it off my boots too." She sighed.

"Try getting it out of fur." He got out of the car and began to strip.

She leaned against it with a grin. "Well, this is fun. Gonna hump my leg, puppy?"

"I usually pee to mark my territory," was his retort before he shifted.

13

SHIFTING into his wolf was strange to do in front of someone, but it would be weirder to ask her to turn around. After all, Brock didn't close his eyes when she vamped out on him.

It didn't take long to change shapes, and the difference was immediate. His sense of smell sharpened, bringing to him a multitude of things to filter from the lingering exhaust of his car to the rubber on his tires to the trees growing nearby. But the one he enjoyed the most?

Hers.

He turned his head toward her. His vision as a wolf was different with colors muted, but at the same time, shapes became sharper, Arianna being the most distinct thing of all.

His mate.

His wolf side had no trouble with the concept. It actually felt smug satisfaction that they'd finally laid claim. A claim he could sense now. She was his.

Want to bet she'd be pissed when she found out? In his defense, he'd expected the whole mating thing would be more difficult and require him biting her or something. Maybe the fact she'd bitten him had done the same trick?

Whatever the case, they were bound. Where she went, he went, and she went into the woods.

She might be wearing heavy boots, but she knew how to move quietly, testing her steps before putting her weight down. She angled her body to avoid branches so that they didn't even sway at her passing. A true predator in motion, which he couldn't help but admire.

He roamed a few yards from her, senses alert for anything out of the ordinary. If they had indeed found the hiding place of Sascha, the experimenting doctor, then he'd most likely have sentries. Brock's job would be to sniff them out so they could avoid them because the last thing they wanted to do was be noticed, especially since they had no idea how many they'd face.

Could be a handful, could be a legion. Gunner claimed in Romania the man had more than a dozen working for him. A dozen wolfmen. Technically doable with princess and her sword.

But what if there were more? He wouldn't risk her.

There was an unnatural silence in the forest. Not a bug dared to buzz. The light breeze didn't penetrate under the thick canopy. He scented no natural wildlife. The usual squirrels, mice, and foxes absent. An indication of something chasing them off—or hunting them to the ground.

The stench hit subtly at first. A whiff that grew stronger. A rancid aroma comprised of fur, rot, and wrong. He couldn't have explained exactly what hit him as off, other than gut instinct. It was also familiar. They'd found a monster similar to the ones plaguing London.

He sidled closer to Arianna to warn, but she knew. She'd drawn her blade and held it ready as she eased forward carefully, her head swiveling left and right.

The attack came from above.

A hairy body dropped from the boughs. She dove to the side even as she slashed, scoring a deep, oozing line that the monster ignored. Just like the one he'd shot in his garage more than a week ago. It was as if they didn't feel pain.

While she kept it occupied with parries and thrusts, her blade a whirling dervish, he pounced from behind, slamming into the creature's legs, causing it to stumble. Arianna didn't waste the opportunity. Her blade swept across and through its neck. The head toppled a few seconds before the body collapsed, the stump gushing ichor.

The putrid smell almost made him gag. He recoiled as did she, her arm over her nose as if it could stop the stench from penetrating.

She muttered, "If I didn't know better, I'd say we just killed a zombie wolfman."

A glance at the head had him agreeing with one caveat: zombie wolfman *bat*. The massive, pointed ears and the snub nose weren't wolf in origin. Definitely one of the hybrid monsters.

She grimaced at the body. "We have to hide this in case a patrol comes by."

He chuffed. Not in disagreement, because while he didn't smell anything other than the beast in this area of the woods, if it were found, a decapitated monster would warn the others of a threat.

The problem? There was nowhere good to hide the body. No ravine or cave, so Arianna did something odd. She put the head back by the body and then grabbed hold of a dead tree. She yanked, snapping the dry trunk, and jumped out of the way before it crashed on the corpse.

She dusted her hands and smiled. "When a tree falls in the forest, does anyone care if it kills a monster?"

He managed a wolfy snort.

She grinned. "I know it's brilliant. We should get it put on a mug."

He shook his shaggy head, but he couldn't help but be pleased. She'd used the word "we."

"Shall we continue, puppy?"

They set off once more, even more cautious than before. They were obviously in the right place, meaning there would be more of the creatures.

A smart protector would have asked her to turn around and taken her somewhere safe. Given he'd like to A) keep his head and B) have sex with her again, he instead followed by her side, respecting her as a warrior. His own fault for falling for a woman of strength and courage.

The human sentry they encountered next proved easy to avoid. He sat in a tree, smoking a cigarette. Even if he were Lycan, the smoke would make it difficult for him to smell anyone sneaking up on him. But smell was the least of their problems. They needed him to not be looking for a minute.

She had her hand on the hilt of a dagger. Most likely thinking of tossing it and either killing or knocking out the sentry.

Bad idea.

Brock nudged the crouched Arianna.

She glanced at him.

In this form, he couldn't speak, but what about the

bond between them? He tried to convey his idea by thinking it hard at her. *Whammy him.*

A frown tugged her brow.

He stared and tried again. *Use your mojo.*

Her lips pursed, and she eyed the fellow in the tree ahead of them. She stood and strolled toward it casual like, not being quiet.

The sentry leapt from the tree, rifle cradled in his arms. "Yo there, honey. You shouldn't be in these woods." The man tossed his cigarette to the ground, the lit ember causing a dried leaf to flare.

Idiot. This was how forest fires started.

"Don't call me honey," she purred, and despite it not being tuned toward Brock, he felt the compulsion in it. "As a matter of fact, don't say anything at all unless I tell you to."

The guy stood slack-jawed.

"What's your name?" she asked.

"Benoit."

"What are you doing here, Benoit?"

"Keeping an eye out for intruders."

"And if you find some, then what?"

"Bring them to the doc."

Brock sidled closer, unable to speak, but he listened intently.

"Tell me about this doc," she encouraged.

"Dr. Sascha needs subjects for his serum."

"What serum?" she prodded, as the man kept his answers short.

"The one that makes us into super soldiers."

She glanced at Brock. Confirmation.

"Are you one of these soldiers?"

The guy nodded.

"Do you change into a wolf?"

"I'm more than that." Benoit's chest puffed out.

"More how?" She kept teasing the answers out.

His brow furrowed. "Who are you?"

She pursed her lips before murmuring, "He's fighting the compulsion." Her stare intensified. "How many people does this doctor have working for him?"

Benoit shook his head and scowled. "What are you doing to me?"

"Go to sleep." She pushed the suggestion, and for a second, the man's eyes fluttered as if he'd obey.

But then they flared, flashing with an unnatural light that coincided with his suddenly sprouting fur as his body and face reshaped.

"Intruder," Benoit growled. He opened his mouth wide as if he'd give warning, only nothing emerged because Arianna proved faster with the blade.

Another head went flying, and she wiped her sword on his body before huffing, "He shouldn't have been able to fight off my commands like that."

Brock didn't do anything to remind her that he had.

153

Perhaps it was a Lycan thing. Then again, it had partially worked. He'd kept his mouth shut for a long fucking time, after all.

She didn't bother hiding the body this time. No point. Once the shift changed, a missing sentry would be noticed no matter what. If he thought she'd turn around, though, he was mistaken.

A grim Arianna kept going, heading for the hum of a generator. He flanked her, watching for any other guards. They found two. He pounced the one with his back to the forest and crushed his throat before he could give warning. She handled the next with a dagger punched through his chest into the heart. While their blood stank, it was nothing like that of the monster they'd killed, implying the serum Benoit mentioned worked differently in some subjects.

The area around the mansion was dark, and yet there were signs of life. It wasn't just the humming generator, but the peeks of light coming from the ruins that the canvas cover openings couldn't completely hide.

At least she knew better than to storm it. She crouched on the edge of the clearing, the vegetation chopped and churned to provide parking for a few vehicles, including a luxury sedan that seemed out of place.

As they watched, several people emerged from the

building, one of them in a lab coat, his features and scar clearly illuminated, flanked by obvious soldiers with guns. But it was the guy in the suit that drew his attention.

He seemed familiar somehow. His skin pale in contrast to his dark hair.

Beside him, Arianna stiffened. She put a hand on his fur and clenched it in warning. They were still as could be as the well-dressed man left in the luxury car. The scientist in the white coat went back inside, as did one of his soldiers. The other eyed the woods, his gaze tracking over their spot without stopping, and yet no doubt he sensed something amiss. Once he went into the ruin, Arianna gave Brock a tug, and they retraced their steps to the car, her agitation clear.

He shifted the moment they came in sight and, as he dressed, said, "That was definitely the doctor Gunner told me about." The scar was distinctive. "I didn't recognize the guy in the suit, though."

"I did," she huffed. "And it's bad."

"Bad how?"

"Because it appears my almost-fiancé is a traitor."

14

ARIANNA COULDN'T HIDE her shock at seeing Luis at that abandoned mansion in the woods. The man had been ardently courting her this past year. And by ardent, she meant negotiating with her father, sending her nice gifts, escorting her to events. During that time, he'd been an utter gentleman to the point she'd point-blank asked him if theirs would be an alliance in name only.

His reply? *"I am not one to jump into entanglements. After all, when one has centuries, what's a few months or years?"* And when she'd then followed up with, *"Are you bothered by my face?"* A query asked with her mask removed for his view only, he'd stared at her and stated simply, *"I am more concerned with the content of your character, as it will outlast physical beauty."* A non-answer but she'd accepted it at the time. Now she saw it for the bullshit he'd been using to infiltrate the flock.

As Brock drove, she ranted aloud, "I can't believe he's been lying this entire time."

"You don't think he wants the alliance?"

"He wants something all right, but I'll wager it's not my hand in marriage," she snarled.

"You're upset. Don't tell me you cared for the guy?" A growled question that matched the white knuckles clenching the steering wheel.

"Calm your jealousy down, puppy. I had no interest in him that way. I always saw it more as a business merger. It stings to know he fooled me so that he could use me." It just proved yet again that she couldn't trust people, except for her father, and maybe... She glanced at Brock, a man who'd stuck by her side despite the danger. Who saw her, all of her, and gained nothing but strife by being with her.

"Look on the positive side," he drawled. "His actions have set you free. Now you won't have to be nice about breaking things off."

"Fuck being nice," she snapped. "The bastard is conspiring with the enemy and is behind the attacks on the flock." A reminder that led to her digging out her phone. "My father needs to know."

The phone call went to voicemail, and something this important couldn't be left as a message. She managed a terse, "Call me back. It's important." Paused and added, "Trust no one."

She hung up and couldn't sit still in the car. She tapped her thighs in agitation.

"What do you think Augustus will do?" Brock drove through the dark, a calm and steady presence.

"He'll kill him." Of that there wasn't even a doubt.

"Luis is the heir to the Seville flock. Won't that cause issues?"

"He's a traitor to our kind. Not only has he been lying to us, he's done something even worse."

"Worse than killing Vampires?"

"Yes," she hissed. "I knew there was something abnormal about those creatures."

"Other than the fact they shouldn't exist?" he retorted sarcastically.

"It's more than that." She turned to eye his profile. "Your friend said they fought wolfmen in Romania, right?"

"According to Gunner, yes."

"And those wolfman had no bat traits, no putrid scents, and no gag-worthy rotting smell when killed?"

"I'd have to ask him, but I'm sure he would have mentioned it if that were the case. What does this have to do with your ex-fiancé?"

"Everything, because I believe he's been supplying the mad doctor with the Vampire genome." A crime so heinous there wasn't technically a law against it because no one would have ever fathomed one of their kind would stoop so low.

"Those things weren't like Vampires, though," Brock pointed out.

"That's because we've evolved past the beast stage of our ancestors."

"Hold on a second. Are you saying Vampires used to be bats?"

"Yes." Her reply was terse. "We used to change to feed until our bodies began adapting."

"Does this mean you can shift?"

"No."

"Are you sure those monsters are part vamp? Because I thought you said they had some zombie traits given their rotting blood."

"Zombie, ghoul, call it what you like. It's what happens to a host when the Vampire genome fails to take properly. The body lives and dies at the same time, rotting from within, driving the host mad with a hunger that can't be assuaged until the putrefaction goes too far and they literally collapse. Usually though, they are killed given the danger they pose."

"Why would fuck face encourage that kind of thing?" Brock tapped the steering wheel. "I mean, what advantage is there to helping this doctor make zombie-bat-wolf monsters?"

"Imagine the army they could create if they got it right. Wolfmen with wings who would kill without qualm to feed their hunger. They might even be able to mesmerize their foes. Imagine how difficult they'd be to stop."

"If that's true, why tip their hand and have their creations reveal themselves by attacking prematurely?"

"Because Luis used our issues with the monsters as part of his pitch," she grumbled. "He offered an alliance that would result in being able to call upon each other in the event of an attack. My father was thinking of accepting so that we could combine our forces and hunt out the monster nest."

"Which would have given him the invitation needed to bring his army right into the flock's midst, allowing him to perform a coup." He whistled. "Damn."

"Damn indeed."

"Following that logic, they went after you to try and force Augustus' hand."

"And badly miscalculated," she said grimly.

"This is big," he muttered. "The Cabal corrupted from within. And now one of the bigger flocks as well."

"The bigger danger isn't even from them but the possibility of exposure. With each attack, the risk of being discovered grows. If that happens, Lycan and Vampire will be at risk."

"I don't think the people making monsters are worried about that."

"I agree, meaning their plot is bigger even than taking over my father's flock. Imagine if they could change humanity with a few injections."

"No one would be safe."

"Some would. After all they'd still have to eat. But humans with nothing to offer would become nothing more than cattle." A dire prediction.

The hour grew late as they pulled into the cottage. Its shutters remained closed with no sign of anything being disturbed.

They entered, and she wanted nothing more than to have a hot shower. She wasn't alone.

Brock joined her, his hands soapy and firm as he skimmed them over her body, a reminder that, despite everything that had happened, they were alive, alert to the danger, and determined to put a stop to it. She had no doubt he'd fight by her side. And possibly die.

A thought she couldn't bear having just admitted to herself. She loved him. Fuck the consequences.

At the same time, who knew how many more moments they'd have?

She turned in his wet embrace to kiss him, her passion fierce. Their lips mashed, and their teeth clanged as they were rough and frantic in their kissing. His hands gripped and lifted her, pressing her back into the cold tile of his shower. As if she cared. The rest of her burned. Only for him did she ignite.

Her legs wrapped around his hips, locking him tight, drawing him into her. He filled her. Stretched her. Pleasured her as he thrust in and out. Slamming her hard enough she clawed his back.

"I will keep you safe," he vowed as he brought her to the brink.

She made her own silent promise against his skin as her lips teased the curve of his neck and shoulder. *I'll find a way for us to be together.*

Because she no longer wanted to imagine a life without him. Didn't want to endure another ten years of longing and pretending.

Together they came, her mouth biting his flesh at the moment of orgasm, an orgasm extended as he bit her back.

Claiming her.

She knew how it worked with Lycans, and she reveled in his mark. They belonged to each other, and no one, not Luis, or a mad doctor, or even Vampire rules, would keep them apart.

They emerged from the shower quiet but not the bad kind. Something had changed between them for the better.

As they dressed, he spoke in a low tone. "Gunner should be arriving today. But I don't know if he'll be enough. I am going to try and contact Quinn as well."

"Once my father knows, he'll want to be a part of any attack," she reminded.

"If there's anything left after sundown."

"Excuse me? Since when was the plan to attack during the day?" He knew she couldn't be outside.

"If these creatures are part vampire, then hitting them in daylight will give us the best odds."

A good point since the putrid monsters never attacked while the sun was out. However... "Not all of them have a problem with the sun. Or have you forgotten our masked attackers?"

"I haven't. At the same time, I have to wonder if those hoods they wore were to protect them."

"I don't think you should do anything until we get a clearer idea of their numbers. We already know they're willing to use deadly force."

"Knowing Gunner, he'll bring the firepower. And I'm not without my own weapons." He winked. "But another reason we need to move fast, as in today, is because those dead sentries will most likely spook them. We can't let them relocate, or we might not find them again."

That was the best argument he could have made. Even as she hated the idea of him going without her. "I'm surprised you're willing to leave me alone."

He grimaced. "That's the one part of the plan I'm not crazy about. The good news is they have no idea we're here."

As if his words were a catalyst, what sounded like tiny bells tinkled outside.

He stiffened. "Someone's in the yard. Get your weapons."

"Could be a rodent or a cat?" she offered as she strapped on her sword and daggers.

"It's possible," he murmured.

It had to be driving him nuts he couldn't look out a window. Her fault. The thick shutters were supposed to protect her from accidental daylight, but now they acted as a detriment to seeing if they had company.

"I'm going to take a look," he stated.

"Where's your gun?"

His lips pursed. "Too loud. The sound will carry, and we don't want anyone showing up, not this close to dawn."

Always worrying about her. "I'm not letting you go out there alone."

She half expected him to argue. His face certainly creased as if he wanted to object, but in the end, he nodded. Good. Because no way would she sit inside like some tit on a bull, waiting to see what happened.

"I'll go out the front. You take the back."

She nodded and headed for the second entrance

off the kitchen. A solid wooden door. She pressed her ear to it and listened.

No sign of anyone on the other side. She didn't detect a heartbeat. She heard the door opposite her opening as Brock exited, and she followed, the backside of the cottage offering a small garden area she'd not actually explored. The rose bushes and other foliage were in hibernation for spring. The fence encircling the yard stood only waist high and proved more decorative than anything. She stood still and listened. Heard nothing. Sensed no one. Smelled nothing. Surely if a monster lurked, its stench would give it away?

But then she thought of the guard they'd killed. He'd indicated he'd been changed, and he didn't reek. What if the successful versions didn't stink?

On instinct, she whirled to glance overhead just as a body swooped down. She yelled. "'Ware the sky!"

The reply from Brock? A howl and a snarl.

She dodged the creature that flew in with wings that actually worked and tucked into its back. While it had the appearance of other monsters with its oversized leathery ears, flat nose, and furry body, it didn't have the same madness in its gaze. And it spoke.

"Surrender."

She arched a brow. "I don't think so."

"Then die."

"We'll see about that," she muttered.

The creature lunged at her, reaching with its claws, and she parried by slicing with her sword. It hissed as she scored a line across its hand instead of taking the fingers.

She twirled her blade. "Come on, big guy. You wanted to play."

It reached for something at its side, and her eyes widened as it pulled a gun from a holster.

Not just any gun, a tranquilizer she realized. Oh shit.

Her turn to dodge as it fired, and she screamed a warning, "They're trying to knock us out."

Try being the key word. She had a resistance to most drugs, and yet she had to wonder if they used a normal human blend or something special concocted by the doctor.

A rustling from behind drew her attention, and she half glanced to see a second flying monster arriving, not as smoothly as the first. His stumble allowed her to duck and whirl, kicking out a foot to slap him in the ankle. As the second beast lost his balance, she thrust, scoring a hit on its leg.

Not enough to dissuade him from showing her his fangs and reaching with both clawed hands. She rolled and popped back upright, spinning like a dervish, relying on her sharp blade to stop anything from getting close.

She didn't get slashed, but something pricked her. A glance down showed a tufted capsule sticking out of her leg.

Fuck. She ignored the tranq to run for the first monster, putting him on defense, forcing him to lift his arms to protect himself, allowing her to slash through the hand holding the weapon. It fell to the ground just as she got pricked in the back.

With a low growl of annoyance, she whirled and went after the second beast, who met her charge by ducking low at the last second and slamming into her legs. She couldn't stop herself from falling backward and hit the ground hard, her head slamming off it, dazing her for a second. The creature sat atop her and grabbed hold of her arms, pinning them to the ground, making her helpless for his friend, who'd recovered his weapon from his chopped hand to use in his remaining one. He fired it point-blank right into her shoulder.

It didn't hurt, but with three injections, the effect had her feeling woozy. Not good. She didn't want to be incapacitated.

She bucked, pulling her legs up and using them to shove the monster off her. She sprang to her feet, her head taking a moment before it joined her, leaving her slightly dizzy.

A sharp cry of pain distracted her. Brock! She had no time to go see or help, as she had her own difficulties. The monsters she'd fought before were easy to defeat. Beasts with no skill, just savage attack. But these... These were the soldiers that must be the goal. Clear-eyed, strong, wily, and working together to come at her from all sides, darting in to slash, distracting her from the left while the right attacked.

It led to her being sliced all over, her blood flowing faster than she could heal, which caused her strength to falter. The monsters pressed in against her, and she heard a snarl before a hairy wolf slammed into one of the beasts engaging her.

It gave her the adrenaline to bounce to her feet, find her fallen sword, and slash anew. She took an arm off one of the super monsters. But it didn't stop it from attacking, as if it felt no pain.

Amidst Brock's snarls of rage, she suddenly heard a voice. A familiar one with a mocking tone she'd never endured in the past.

"If it isn't the Lord Augustus' daughter and heir." She whirled to see Luis approaching, looking calm and smug.

"You!" She pointed her sword, doing her best to control her tremble. "Traitor."

"According to you. I see myself more as a man with vision, a better one than your father. Once I take his place—"

"Never." She lunged, only to trip as a beast literally threw itself at her feet.

She hit the ground hard, her grip never faltering on her sword, leading to bruised fingers when she landed. She pushed herself up on her arms as Luis continued to drawl.

"As I was saying, once I remove your father, the flock will fall into line and call me lord. After all, they don't care who leads them so long as they get their blood."

"You won't get away with this." She pushed herself to her knees.

"I already have. Your lover is sleeping and won't be able to perform a heroic rescue." A quick glance showed Brock lying prone on the ground. "And hadn't you wondered why your father wasn't answering?"

She blinked. "You killed my daddy?" She sounded like a lost little girl because, in that moment, she was. Her father was supposed to be invincible.

"As we speak, your flock is being given a choice. Serve me or face the dawn."

"That's not a choice," she huffed, using her anger to fight the tears.

"And yet, it's the same one I will offer you. Bow before me and swear fealty, or..." He glanced to the sky. "Won't be long now before the sun rises. What will it be?"

"Why don't you come a little closer and ask me again," she taunted as she rose to her feet, the drug in her veins doing its best to put her to sleep. Only her strong will kept her upright.

"If you insist."

As he began to move, the monsters rushed her and grabbed hold of her arms, pinning her in place. Struggling didn't free her. Not with her strength depleted.

Luis smirked in front of her. "Not so haughty now, are you, Lady Arianna?"

"Coward," she spat.

"I prefer to think of it as smart. A good leader doesn't take chances. You know what else he doesn't do? Leave loose ends."

He angled his head, and the pressure on her wrist made her lose her grip on her sword. A sword he picked up and pointed at Arianna.

"Just so you know, I lied when you asked if I could stand your hideous face. As if I'd tie myself to someone defective like you. The person who stands by my side should be a complement to me, not an ugly distraction."

And with that insult, he ran her through with her own sword. The monsters released her, and she slumped to the ground, bleeding heavily. Hurting even more. Not because of her wounds but because she could do nothing as they dragged an unconscious wolf, peppered in darts, past her. She crawled after them. She had to save Brock.

The will was there, but the ability wasn't. She collapsed in the front yard and could only listen as they tossed Brock into the trunk of the car Luis had arrived in. The surviving monsters took to the sky while Luis drove off with Brock, leaving her for dead.

Dawn approached, and Arianna lacked the strength to move. But she tried. She pushed to her knees to crawl, only to collapse. She couldn't give up. She slithered, dragging herself bit by bit for the safety of the cottage. If she could make it to shadow, she might survive until nightfall. A good hunt would help her heal.

A crunch of gravel had her turning her head to see a car stopping out front. A man stepped out and gasped. "What the fuck happened? Who are you? Where's Brock?"

"He's gone," she slurred.

"You killed him?"

"Never," she spat through blood frothing lips. "They took him."

"Who?"

Rather than reply, she hissed as the peeking sun hit her skin. It didn't hurt, not yet, but that might be because of her injuries.

"You're a vampire." Stated flatly.

"No shit," she muttered, wondering if he'd stop her from attempting to crawl the last few feet into the house.

"Lady Arianna, I presume?" He didn't wait for an answer. "Let's get you inside." He scooped her and carried her into the cottage, where she passed out.

15

ARIANNA WOKE to warm blood filling her mouth, whose she didn't know, didn't care. The hunger gnawed at her something fierce, and so she gulped hungrily, mewling in annoyance when a stern voice said, "Enough, Nina. Don't you dare drain Bernie to death."

She had to be dreaming because that sounded like her father, but Luis said he'd been killed.

"Daddy?" She said his name weakly and, when he came into her blurry view, promptly burst into tears. "You're not dead," she sobbed.

"Not for a lack of trying."

"How?" she asked,

"Later. Rest. You must be strong for our revenge."

Vengeance. Yes. Because Luis had taken Brock.

With blood to help fuel her, she fell into a proper healing sleep.

When she next woke, she felt stronger, the pain of her wounds almost gone. She rose from the bed in the cottage basement in confusion. She'd dreamed her father had come. Impossible since he was dead.

Or was he?

Going upstairs, she heard the murmur of voices and emerged to find her father present, along with Bernie—looking impeccable in his tweed suit, if incongruous bearing a shotgun—and another man, dressed in jeans and plaid, layered with a vest. Vaguely familiar but not as interesting as the man who came to her rescue.

Tears of happiness pricked her eyes. "Daddy, it is you."

He turned to her with a smile. "Nina, about time you woke."

She ran for him, not caring how it looked but wanting his arms around her, proving he lived. He hugged her hard, murmuring, "My sweet, Nina, I thought I'd lost you."

"I was told you were dead."

"Ha, as if I would be so easy to kill," Augustus scoffed.

"Luis betrayed us."

"I know." A dark and stark statement. "He will pay for that."

"What are you doing here? Who is this?" She eyed the stranger who'd saved her life. Had he not brought her inside, she'd have barbecued.

The man held out his hand. "Gunner. An army mate of Brock's."

She took his offered limb and gave it a firm squeeze and shake. "Arianna. Thank you for coming to my aid."

"I'll admit, I didn't expect to ever save a Vampire from daylight." He shook his head. "But knowing Brock, he would have been peeved at me if I hadn't."

"He mentioned you were coming."

"Did he also mention the fact I told him to wait before poking his nose into things? I told him Sascha and his fucking creations were dangerous."

She grimaced. "My fault. We went scouting to find out where they were holed up."

"I take it you found them."

She nodded and added, "And they then turned around and found us right back. They ambushed us and took Brock."

"Luis left you behind?" A surprised exclamation by her father.

She shrugged. "He said I'd be an impediment to his takeover. He's the one who stabbed me after his monsters drugged me. If not for Gunner's timely arrival, I'd be dead."

"But why take Brock?" Her father sounded confused.

Gunner had a reply. "I'm thinking they needed fresh blood to play with since we shut down Sascha's operation in Romania. Don't forget, while Brock never took a position in a pack, he's got alpha blood in his veins."

"Meaning they're going to use him to make more of their monsters." Her lip curled. "Luis has been helping the scientist behind it. He's given them some of his genome to modify their test subjects into almost unstoppable beasts."

"Creating an army. So I discovered too late." Her father grimaced. "It was only by chance I wasn't caught in the invasion at the compound. Bernie and I were in the wine cellar when they attacked. Given how quickly they captured the upper floors, he and I fled through the secret tunnels."

"What of the rest of the flock?" she asked.

Her father's lips turned down. "Some died trying to stand against them. A few escaped. From the surveillance footage I had access to before they shut off the cameras, it appears the rest agreed to serve Luis as their new master."

"Spineless cowards," she huffed.

"The flock might be clever, but they're not warriors like you. Given the choice between life or death, what would you choose to do?"

"Fight," she snapped. "Your court is useless."

"I'm aware." His dry reply.

"So what are we going to do?" she asked.

"Find a way to kill Luis of course."

"Ahem, if I may?" Gunner interjected. "While I understand you want revenge, if we don't rescue Brock and quickly, who knows what damage they'll do to him."

"Oh, I hadn't forgotten about him," she stated. "The headquarters they created in the ruins is about a thirty-or-so-minute drive from here. But if we're going to get in and retrieve him, we'll need help. While some of their monsters are simple to beat, the ones I faced last night were next level."

"Then it's a good thing I brought firepower." And by that Gunner meant he'd managed to acquire a trunk full of weapons. Semi-automatic rifles. Handguns. Even some grenades. What they lacked? Enough hands to wield them.

She paced the cottage. "We need more people."

Bernie cleared his throat and raised his hand. "I can shoot."

She eyed Bernie, who was more than a blood

donor. He'd been her father's friend and confidant for a long time. "It will be dangerous."

Bernie offered a rueful smile. "I live with Vampires. Every day is perilous." A reminder that not all donors survived the sharing of blood. Some of the younger Vampires lacked control over their hunger. Other donors just couldn't handle the requirements.

Her father nodded. "Thank you, old friend. Your aid is appreciated."

Four of them against who knew how many, and them stuck until nightfall given the sun outside. The cottage remained shuttered against the sun, and yet her father didn't flinch when he passed through a stray beam of light coming in through a crack. With age, and increased ability, came a resistance to the ill effects of the sun. She wondered if she'd live long enough to enjoy that same perk.

That would depend on today's outcome because she wasn't giving up the fight until Brock was freed and Luis, along with his evil doctor ally, was dead.

When Gunner exited the cottage to make some phone calls to try and wrangle help from someone named Quinn, she took the opportunity to question her father.

"Why did Luis sound so sure you were dead?"

"Most likely whoever he sent mistook Pierrot for me. He was in my office when they attacked." Pierrot being his personal assistant. While Luis would have known the difference, the monster soldiers wouldn't.

"I'm surprised you came looking for me instead of trying to take back the compound."

Her father grimaced. "I thought about it, but let's be honest, you're my best fighter. And once I realized the perfidy, my concern was more for you than anyone else."

"But Brock never told you where we went."

Her father shifted before sighing. "I've been tracking your phone since you left."

"I thought my phone was tracker proof."

"To everyone else, maybe."

"How come you didn't answer when I called?" she accused.

"I was busy escaping at the time, and the tunnels had no signal. By the time I emerged, I had dawn to contend with, and you weren't answering."

"Because I was passed out." Her nose wrinkled. "Do you think they'll harm Brock? He's been in their custody for hours."

"You like him." Stated, not asked.

"He's a good man," she hedged.

"He's also a Lycan."

"And?" she riposted. "I don't understand this whole schism between our kind. He's a good guy and should be judged on that, not the fact he shifts into a wolf."

"I agree he's a great man. I'd even call him a friend and someone I would trust in a crisis. Obviously since I sent him off with you. In my haste to get you safe, I forgot to warn you, though."

"About?"

"Lycan blood."

"You mean the rumors of it tasting bad?"

"It's more than a rumor. Vampires can't ingest it."

She frowned. "What are you talking about?" And then because there was no point in hiding it. "It's too late. I've already partaken of his blood." She didn't announce he was delicious and eating him was better than anything she'd ever had.

Her father blinked. "You've drank from him?"

"Numerous times."

He eyed her up and down. "And how do you feel?"

"Fine. Why?"

Her father's mouth rounded. "I'll be damned. That's unexpected."

"What is?"

"The fact he's your mate."

She blinked. "Er, what?" How had he guessed when she and Brock hadn't even admitted it aloud yet?

"Guess I should have known with the way you were always finding excuses to see him."

"I'll have you know we only started sharing blood and stuff"—she did her best to not blush—"after the attack. I was wounded, and he wanted to help."

"You're lucky he's your mate, or you would have regretted it."

"Explain."

"I know you've wondered why there's a ban on Lycans and Vampires associating. It's simple really." Her father spread his hands. "Lycan blood is toxic to Vampires, as in undigestible. While it doesn't kill the strong, it is very unpleasant in flavor and causes immediate gastric upset that may result in the spewing of bodily fluids."

"Vampires don't puke." They might expel waste like humans, but they were never sick. Even the drunkest Vampire could just sleep it off.

"They do on Lycan blood."

"I don't."

"So a not well-known fact is a mated Vampire and Lycan don't have any issues."

"We were strangers the first time I bit him, though."

"Doesn't matter, you were fated to be. Making his blood the only Lycan blood you can tolerate."

"Seriously? How is this the first I've heard of it?"

"Because a mated pair is rare. Don't forget, you've known all your life not to eat the dog. Right?"

"He's not a dog," she muttered, trying to ignore her nickname for him.

"Obviously. You wouldn't be mated to someone weaker than you. And don't forget, I know Brock. I've called him friend for a long time."

"You don't sound as if you're mad we're mated." It felt odd saying it aloud since she'd not really done so with Brock. But at the same time, having her father confirm what she suspected helped.

"Mad? What would anger do but drive a wedge between us? And I don't think this mating is a bad thing, even if some are threatened."

"Threatened how?"

"Because a bond between a Vampire and Lycan is like no other. You'll have to explore the extent of it, as it varies from couple to couple."

She already had a few examples, such as the way Brock resisted her mesmerizing, and how he'd spoken into her head the previous night in the woods. What else could they do together?

"The flock won't like it. You know how they act when you have Brock over."

"You mean how they scatter in disapproval," her father mocked.

"They'll demand you banish me at the very least."

"They can demand all they like. They're cowards and would rather kneel than fight." Her father arched a brow. "If I choose to rescue them, then the flock can either accept my daughter and her Lycan mate or find somewhere else to live."

"You say that, and yet we both know it's not that simple."

"You're my daughter. You come above everyone else." A low promise and she knew he meant it.

She hugged him. To think she'd worried he'd be upset with her choice.

"We'll figure something out," she swore.

Gunner walked in at that moment and waved his phone. "We can't expect any help. No one's anywhere close, but I've got a plan."

"Let's hear it," she asked.

It proved simple. They would put in a call to local law enforcement about a meth lab at the abandoned Baron Hill Manor. The police raid would cause chaos, and most likely the beasts would scatter into the woods, where they'd be waiting to pick them off.

At least Gunner and Bernie would. She and her father would sneak into the ruins and grab Brock, escaping in the chaos. If they saw the doctor or Luis, they'd kill them. If they somehow escaped, they'd track them down once they'd rescued and regrouped with Brock.

It would have worked better if the mansion hadn't been abandoned while she slept all day.

The police ran through the place, screaming and calling all-clears. They found signs of the tarped-over ruins being used as a lab. In their haste, Sascha and his goons left some of the medical equipment behind. But of Brock there was no sign. No clue as to where he'd been taken.

She might have been more despondent if, as they sped off from the ruins of disappointment, Bernie didn't clear his throat to announce, "Darby texted me."

"Darby's alive?" Arianna exclaimed. The compound's housekeeper had been around a good portion of her life and made the best blood pudding and sausage.

"She is in good health, and she just let me know that Luis is currently in residence with his monstrous army and that some doctor has taken up residence in the north wing."

"What of Brock?" she asked.

Bernie texted quickly. Within seconds, he shrugged. "Darby says she didn't see him, sorry."

Chances were good, though, that if he lived, he'd be with the doctor.

Arianna eyed her dad. "Time to take back our home."

16

NOTHING LIKE WAKING up strapped to a gurney. Brock blinked a few times, trying to get his bearings. He appeared to be in a luxurious bedroom with an intricate ceiling and a hanging chandelier.

A tug of his arms showed his wrists bound, his ankles too. There was a strap over his chest and another across his forehead, keeping him from even turning for a side peek.

Bad sign given his last recollection was of him fighting those bat-wolfmen monsters. They'd obviously taken him prisoner. But what of Arianna?

He couldn't smell or sense her nearby. He bucked and thrashed uselessly.

"At last, you're awake. Took you long enough," was the grumbled complaint before a visage leaned over him.

He didn't recognize the older man with his buzzed almost-white hair. He had a scar that traversed his entire face. Silvery and ridged. Somehow, he'd kept his eyes.

"Who are you?" Brock asked.

"As if you can't guess. I would have thought your friend Gunner would have told you all about me by now."

"You're that doctor. Sascha something or other."

"Give the dog a prize." The doctor leered in mockery. "Hard to believe you're supposed to be an alpha."

The man tried to rile him, but Brock didn't fall for it. "Where's Arianna?"

"Who?" the doctor asked.

"The woman I was with."

"No idea. You'd have to ask Luis. He was the one who captured you for me. I have to say, had I known how good your genetics would turn out to be, I would have acquired you sooner."

"What?" The word "genetics" made his blood run cold.

"I consider it poetic justice in a sense. Your friend ruined my research and lab in Romania. All those lovely samples gone. But then I remembered him mentioning his friend in London. And what do you know, that friend isn't just a wolf mutt like the others but an alpha." The man appeared almost gleeful. "Oh, the things I can do with you."

It turned Brock's blood to ice. "Release me." A useless demand to make and yet he still asked.

"I don't think so. I've gone to a lot of trouble to capture you. Do you know how rare it is to find an alpha these days? Especially since I broke the ones I had." His lips turned down. "Science can be such a difficult thing. Test after test. Tweak after tweak. But at least I think I've found the combination."

"To what?" Brock found himself morbidly curious.

"You'll see," the crazy doctor sang as he disappeared from sight, but he remained in the room. Brock could hear him, moving around, pouring liquids. Making machines hum. The clink of glass.

The needle full of a murky liquid that suddenly appeared in his line of sight made his heart stutter.

"What is that?"

"The next step in evolution."

Before the doctor could inject the liquid, a shrill female voice cried out. "What are you doing?"

The mad doctor glanced over his shoulder and offered a flat, "Starting the protocol."

"We talked about waiting." The woman's heels clacked as she neared.

"That was before we lost even more of the Vamplyc." As if sensing Brock's bafflement at the word, the doctor turned to offer him a smug smirk. "It's what I've called the meld of Lycan and Vampire."

"It's a terrible name," he blurted out.

"We're also testing Lympire."

Brock grimaced. "Even worse."

"Vamwolf?"

"How about you don't mix the two? Like, why would you even do that?"

"Why not? The best of both species intertwined together brings us to the next level of being." The man looked positively beatific as he spouted his nonsense. "Unfortunately, the protocol doesn't work with just anyone. You should count yourself lucky. Only the strong survive the treatment."

"No treatment!" The woman who'd yelled out moments before came close enough he could see the single hair on her chin. "We talked about keeping him untouched."

"Ah yes, you and your 'let's breed him.'" The man waved the needle around.

"It makes sense to extract his seed for future use. None of this messy letting them procreate on their own anymore. We will find suitable females to impregnate that we might harvest their fetuses and apply the accelerated growth serum. We need more Lycans loyal to us if your plan is going to work."

What plan? Brock listened rather than asked. Might as well find out all he could before he escaped.

Because he would escape.

"Growing specimens from scratch takes so long," Sacha groaned.

"Then force the alpha to make more. After all, isn't that how you created this one in the first place?"

Sascha eyed him. "Frederick made impressive subjects. It was a shame you and your military friends escaped."

"You were the one holding us prisoner?" He still remembered the resignation to his death. He'd been sure so sure he'd never make it out alive.

"I blame the guards. I warned them to keep him in the dark on the full moon. What happened is all on them."

A good thing they'd been negligent, or he might have died there.

"You don't have Fred, but you've got one of his alphas. Use him to make more. Men are easy to find and bribe."

"You know I hate the biting. It's so unscientific," the doctor grumbled.

"And yet what choice do we have? Until we acquire another Lycan-born female, we won't be able to recreate the serum that changes them into your wolfman soldiers."

A good thing Gunner had already told him of this sick experiment, or he might have been more shocked.

"Fine. I will wait," huffed by a disgruntled doctor. "Have the refrigeration units arrived yet?" The needle hit a tray, and Sascha left with the woman.

Brock didn't remain alone for long.

A man entered, smelling distinctly of Lycan. His salt-and-pepper hair was slicked back. He wore a suit jacket over a button shirt, but no tie. He stood over Brock with a frown. "This wasn't what I signed up for, just so you know."

It made no sense. "And you are?"

"Dmitri."

"The Cabal traitor," Brock stated without pause. Gunner had spoken of him. Married to a woman called Joella, sister to Sascha. Most likely she was the woman who'd just left.

The man pursed his lips, making his jowls more pronounced. "I do what I must to ensure our survival. Lycans can't hide in the dark forever, but before we come out, we have to find a way to preserve our lineage."

"From what?"

"Annihilation," Dmitri announced. "The moment the humans discover our existence, our kind will be hunted, unless we have leverage. Imagine their fear if we threatened to turn them all into Lycans if they tried to exterminate us."

"Are you trying to convince me this is altruistic?" Brock couldn't hide his sarcasm. "You are experimenting on your own kind."

"Science needs sacrifice."

"Says the man who gives up nothing. And what of the monsters they've been making? Are those part of your keeping-Lycans-alive plan?"

Dmitri's lips turned even further down. "I had no idea Sascha had been playing with Vampires. I would have never agreed."

"And yet here you are, aiding and abetting. Does the Cabal know just how corrupt you are?"

Dmitri turned away from him. "The Cabal needs to change."

"The Cabal's job is to protect Lycans, not offer them up for experimentation," Brock exclaimed.

"Once I show them results—"

"Do you really think they'll care? Because I sure as fuck don't. What you're doing is depraved."

Dmitri appeared annoyed that Brock didn't fawn over his twisted logic. "I can see you're not ready to listen."

"Kind of hard to see your point of view when I'm the one fucking strapped down!" Brock yelled.

No reply. The slam of the door let him know he was alone.

Or not.

While he heard and smelled nothing, he sensed someone remained in the room.

"Who's there?" No answer. "You might as well stop pretending. I might be tied down tighter than a pig on a spit, but I've still got all my senses."

"Should have known a dog would sniff me out," came the disdainful reply.

"Who are you?" A question he'd asked too much already since he'd woken.

"The one who captured you." A haughty male stood over him, the same one he'd seen at the ruins. "Hard to believe Arianna chose to run away with you. Then again, with her face, I guess she couldn't exactly do better."

The insult had Brock straining. "Don't speak of her like that."

"I will speak of her any way I please, given we were almost engaged. I even contemplated going through with the wedding. After all, it would be easy to kill her once we shared a bed. But the thought of having to pretend any longer— Well, I guess it's a good thing she refused to swear fealty and chose death."

The claim hit Brock hard, and he blurted out, "Arianna's not dead."

"I don't see how she could have lived. Between her wounds, the sleeping agent, the rising sun, and the sword I put through her gut, even if she made it to a dark place, she wouldn't have survived until nightfall without blood."

"Arianna is tough."

"Tough, but not invincible. Vampires are long-lived, not immortal. Grievous wounds, the sun and more can kill."

Brock's heart wanted to break, but at the same time, a part of him didn't believe. Surely he'd know if she died? She was his mate. He'd have felt it.

"I will kill you," he promised.

"That seems unlikely given our plans for you." Luis leaned close enough Brock could smell the blood on his breath. "Count yourself lucky we have need of your genetics, or I'd have already eviscerated you."

"You will pay for everything you've done."

"The sooner you accept you've lost, the better for you. I look forward to when you bend a knee and call me master."

"Never."

"As if you have a choice. I am better than you in all ways. If I command you to do something, you will do it."

"You think you're that strong?" Brock couldn't help

but chuckle. "I dare you to whammy me and then untie these straps."

Luis leaned close, staring into his eyes, and said, "Beg me to suck my cock."

"I'd rather be injected with that poison shit your doctor's been playing with."

The other man's gaze widened in obvious surprise that Brock hadn't succumbed. Apparently, he didn't know that alphas, even those without a pack, could fight the mesmerizing.

Luis recovered to drawl, "Do you fuck her from behind to avoid looking at her face? I can't blame you. It made my dick limp when I saw it."

Brock snarled and heaved, caught by the straps.

Luis chuckled. "Maybe I should have kept her alive. Imagine the fun of you watching me fuck her."

With those haunting words, Luis left.

It killed Brock to realize he might be well and truly fucked. Tied to a gurney. A rat for experimenting to a sadistic doctor. A prisoner for torturing to a fucking power-hungry vampire. And a breeder and maker to an insane bitch.

But the worse thing of all? Luis's claim Arianna was dead.

It couldn't be. He refused to believe it. She was too tough to simply die. He'd have known if it happened. Felt it.

The doctor returned, humming under his breath. The rattle of metal had Brock straining anew. Especially as the doctor wheeled a cart to his side and declared, "Time to fetch your swimmers."

"Keep your hands off my balls."

"If you wolves weren't so obsessed with getting a vasectomy, we could have done this a more pleasant way. But no, your Cabal has you all cowed into submission and so"—the doctor held up a scalpel—"we must cut directly into your scrotum for extraction."

The doctor didn't bother numbing Brock's jewels before pressing the blade to them and slicing.

The pain hit instantly. He wanted to howl, but that would be showing the man weakness. Fuck that. Despite being bound, he did his best to fight. Hips jerked, and his legs twitched.

The doctor grumbled, "You're making a mess."

"Too fucking bad."

The doctor slapped a mask over Brock's face, and Brock accidentally gasped, sucking in some gas. Then he tried holding his breath, even while knowing he couldn't hold out for long. He sucked in and let himself go to sleep.

He came to groggy and to the sound of someone talking low under their breath. "...thinks she can tell me what to do. Well, I've got her precious seed. And I've got enough blood to hold us over for a bit. Now it's my turn. Time to see if you're as strong as you seem."

Brock blinked his eyes, the brightness overhead making him squint.

"Awake already?" A blurry doctor leaned into view. "Should have stayed asleep. This might burn a little." The doctor held up a needle that doubled and tripled.

It sobered Brock quickly into blurting out, "What are you doing? Your sister said no changing me."

"My sister doesn't tell me what to do." The needle went into his arm.

And set him on fire.

His whole body arched, and he screamed.

Screamed as if he were being torn to pieces.

Felt his body swelling and straining at the straps binding him.

Then the mask was over his face again, and he sucked in the sleeping gas, wanting to escape the agony.

Next time he woke, his body was cold, so very, very cold. He could hear arguing, Joella's shrill voice demanding, "How is he supposed to bite the men I've acquired if he's asleep?"

"If you're so keen on making some the old-fashioned way, ask your husband," Sascha replied.

"You know he's grown too weak. If I didn't still

need a voice on the Cabal, I'd have gotten rid of him a while ago," she retorted.

"Maybe it's time he joined the ranks with the others we've changed," Joella's brother offered.

"Go ahead. But leave this one alone."

A door slammed, and the doctor muttered, "You don't get to tell me what to do."

The shuffle of steps brought Sascha close enough Brock could see him through his slitted eyes. He held up a needle, squirting liquid out of the tip to remove air bubbles.

Brock managed a slurred, "What is that?"

"Round two. It takes a minimum of three in quick succession for it to work."

"Don't," Brock pleaded as the needle neared.

"Always with the begging," the doctor muttered, plunging it into Brock's flesh.

The pinprick didn't hurt. The liquid gushed, icy at first, before it started to burn. The fire raced through, up and down his arm, making his fingers spasm. It flowed through his veins, igniting pain into every inch of his body.

He puffed and panted. Straining. Growling.

"Fascinating." The doctor shone a light in his eyes. "You are reacting much differently than the other subjects. I wonder why..."

Pop. Pop. Pop.

Distant gunfire distracted Sascha. He turned from Brock with a frown. "Don't go anywhere. I'm going to see what's happening." The doctor left.

The distant popping stopped. But the fire within grew stronger, and Brock didn't like it. Not one bit. It didn't help he suddenly hungered.

But the food he craved wasn't in this room.

He needed it. Now!

He strained at the ties binding him, and they snapped. He tore himself free of the bed and stood beside it. With a roar, he grabbed it and threw. The crashing noise didn't appease his annoyance, but it did open the door.

A man wearing black camo stared at him. Then the broken bed. "You're not supposed to do that."

Brock didn't fucking care. The beating of the man's heart had him flying across the room. The guard died, his blood a mere snack to the raging emptiness inside.

Brock needed more.

So he went hunting for it.

17

ARIANNA'S ANXIETY knew no bounds. They'd wasted their time the night before raiding a place already emptied. The drive to London took forever, and they were still a few miles outside the compound with dawn fast approaching.

"We're going to have to take cover," she murmured to her father who sat with her in the backseat.

"I'm aware. Patience. Bernie knows where to go."

She could only assume her father had a plan since they barely had enough time to get to ground, literally.

When Bernie parked by a cemetery, Gunner raised a brow. "I know you're considered the living dead, but seriously?"

Her daddy chuckled. "Not many people go nosing around graveyards, especially at night. There's a tunnel entrance in a mausoleum I own."

The revelation caused Arianna to blurt out, "There's a tunnel in our crypt?"

Her father shrugged. "After the attack on our family, I had a few more emergency exits installed."

"I know about those. But none of them emerge in the cemetery," she pointed out.

"Because this one was meant to be a surprise for you."

"I don't understand."

"You'll soon see. Come, let's make haste. Dawn is close." Her father led through them through the cemetery to the family vault constructed almost a century ago during his grief to hold her mother and two siblings. She'd not visited often, too overcome with the guilt of a child who'd been unable to do anything.

The locked door opened with the key her father retrieved from the headstone of a blood donor he'd been fond of. Mario had often bounced her on his knee after a feeding, the old man loving to regale her with stories of the olden days.

Only once the door closed did her father light the candles on the ledge running on either side of the entrance. The flickering flames gave them enough light to see. The inside of the vault didn't have the usual musty smell of most places rarely visited and housing the dead. Her father still visited regularly, judging by the fresh flowers in front of each interment niche.

The flagstone floor appeared normal until he knelt and pressed the letters in her mother's first name backwards. The floor barely made a sound as it dropped and moved sideways, revealing stairs.

Gunner whistled. "This is some next-level shit."

"When did you have this built?" she exclaimed.

"I started it over two years ago. I wanted it in place before I offered you the carriage house to use."

She stared at him. "How did you know I'd want to move out of the house?"

He rolled his shoulders. "I'm your father. I could see you chafed at being under the eye of the court. I figured the carriage house would give you that independence you craved while still offering you the protection of the flock."

"Some protection they turned out to be," she grumbled.

"Okay, so maybe I selfishly wanted to keep you close."

"Could you two be any more gag-worthy lovey-dovey father and daughter?" Gunner complained.

"Spoken by someone who doesn't have love in his life," her father replied.

"More like I lost it," Gunner muttered. Then cleared his throat. "How far is this tunnel?"

"A few hundred yards. It's why it's taken so long to build. It had to be done subtly so no one would notice."

"And you kept telling everyone to stay away from the carriage house because there'd been problems with local kids using it as a make-out spot." People under twenty-one were forbidden as food. No exception. Just like fledgling vamps had to be over twenty-five. Her own father made her wait until twenty-seven to change her. He kept hoping she'd changed her mind and have a child or two first. An heir of her own.

She'd refused and offered to adopt a few cats instead—which he couldn't stand.

They compromised. He brought her over, and rather than cats, she stuck to having expensive hobbies, like classic car restoration.

As they walked through the tunnel of concrete blocks, she had questions. "This goes all the way to the cellar under the carriage house?"

Her father nodded. "When I began the construction, I wanted to be sure you had a way to exit should we ever come under attack."

She flung her arms around her father, who staggered only slightly before squeezing her back.

"I will do anything to keep you safe," he murmured against her hair.

"I know." And she would do the same.

Gunner cleared his throat harshly and wetly. "While this is touching and all..."

"Let us continue. We can rest and regroup once we reach the cellar."

The tunnel ended in a door that her father showed her how to open. The cellar had been transformed from a rough stone-and-dirt dungeon to a heated concrete floor, reinforced walls and ceiling—

"Holy bomb shelter!" Gunner glanced around at the transformed space with wonder. "Damn, I know where I want to stay if the apocalypse hits."

Her father rolled his shoulders. "History has shown the most common way humans have of eliminating our kind is by burning or collapsing our homes atop us. In essence, burying us alive. This provides a layer of protection from that and comes with two exits. The one to the cemetery and another to the pool cabana by the house."

"You know, gotta say, you're not the evil monsters I expected," Gunner admitted. "Guess I'm gonna need to apologize to Brock if I'm gonna get invited to the wedding."

"Wedding?" She grimaced.

Her father, though, beamed. "I still have your mother's dress."

She didn't have the heart to tell him she wasn't the type to walk down the aisle, even if she wanted forever. All those people gawking at her? No thanks.

It was as she passed by a steel support beam, her

reflection just a fuzzy blob with the single lantern light, she realized she hadn't put on a mask. Hadn't even thought of it. Nor had Gunner made mention of her scar or stared.

His reaction and Brock's didn't mean she wouldn't encounter those who would be rude— or worse, pitying. However, perhaps it was past time she wore her scar with pride. After all, according to her father, it proved her strength, and if she listened to Brock, she was beautiful.

As if sensing her pensive mood, her father came near. "Are you all right?"

She canted her head as she lifted a shoulder. "Yes and no." Her injuries had healed, but her anxiety over Brock left her agitated.

"You want to go find him."

"The longer he's in their custody, the more chance they'll do something to him."

"The tunnel from here to the house isn't complete."

"Meaning what?" Gunner asked, lifting his head.

"It's excavated but hasn't been fully reinforced with cinderblocks and a roof support."

"But it goes all the way?" Arianna clarified.

Father nodded. "It emerges in my personal wine cellar, which only you, Bernie, and I have access to."

"If we go now, they won't be expecting us," Arianna stated. It was barely noon.

"How many can we expect to fight?" Gunner asked.

Bernie provided the answer. "Seventeen modified intruders, at least ten humans, and Lord Luis."

"He's no Lord," Father grumbled.

"What of your people?" Gunner paused in the checking of his many weapons.

"The flock aren't fighters." Her lip curled. "It's how the compound fell so easily the first time."

"And if they decide to get in our way?" Gunner questioned as he continued to check his weapons.

"Shoot them," Father replied. "I would recommend in the head. Very hard to heal from."

"I thought Vampires were immortal?" Gunner's confusion showed.

"That's what we like people to think," she replied, choosing to be honest with Brock's friend. "The more powerful a vampire, the harder to kill, but we can die. Grievous blood loss, a head shot that causes too much damage to the brain. Puncturing the heart in such a way that it can't heal. Those might kill but, to be sure, cut off the head."

Gunner glanced at his guns. "I guess that explains your sword."

"If you slow them down, I can handle the rest," she assured him. "The monsters the doctor has been making aren't that easy to kill, though. They don't react to injury, so don't assume anything when fighting them."

"Eleven monsters. Piece of cake. Right, Bernie?" Gunner slapped his back.

The older man looked utterly serious even as he wrapped his tie around his forehead and uttered in a flat voice, "Hasta la vista, baby." She didn't tell him he'd quoted the Terminator while pulling a Rambo bandanna. He always was adorable that way.

Her father rolled up his sleeves and shed his jacket. While he might be over a century, he remained powerful. And angry.

So very, very angry.

He glanced at her. "Ready?"

She nodded. Time to save her mate.

The next tunnel didn't take as long to cross, or so it felt. She had a quick stride as they traversed the rougher section. Parts of it still had visible rock and excavated dirt. It must be costing a fortune to maintain a secret crew to handle the work. Not to mention the mesmerizing to make sure none of them spoke of it.

They emerged in the wine cellar, the space a temperature-controlled maze of racks holding bottles. The door, a solid affair, didn't give visual access to the other side. Father stood by a control panel and typed into it.

"Didn't they take control of the house system?" Gunner asked.

Father chuckled. "They just think they did because they removed the remote access point. But they can't keep me out when I'm inside without shutting it all down." He pulled up some cameras and flipped through them. "There's no one outside the room or in the next two up the hall." He kept skimming camera feeds before stopping and saying, "They appear to be mobilizing in the main hall."

"Against what?" she asked, leaning over for a look.

"Does it matter? If they're distracted, now's our chance," Gunner pointed out.

"He's right. We'll figure it out when we get up there. Maybe it's one of their monster soldiers gone berserk. If that's the case, it will take a few of them out, making our odds even better."

Emerging into the second basement level of the compound, they heard and saw no one. They followed Arianna, who took point, knowing the layout. Despite what her father might say, as his heir, it was her right to act as protector.

They went on light feet swiftly up the hall, reaching the junction. Bernie waved at them and whispered. "I'm going to the control room to meet up with

Darby. She's just given the guy inside some coffee with a sleeping agent in it."

"See if you can lock down some rooms to give us time to handle those in our path," Father asked.

"On it." Bernie left them, and they moved up the first set of stairs, the wide steps empty.

She glanced behind her. "Do you think the flock were locked in their rooms?" Most of them chose to spend the day underground. They had three floors of suites to accommodate them.

"If we're lucky. We don't need them in our way," her father murmured before adding, "Company."

Even as he finished saying it, he sprinted up the steps to throw himself at the man coming down. The guy never had a chance to yell. Her father's arm over his mouth muffled it. But the invading soldier struggled, had even started shifting into his beast, when her father snapped his neck and dropped the body.

He grimaced at it. "That's disturbing."

"What is?" she asked, nearing enough to see the body looked semi shifted.

"A second ago, it smelled human."

She inhaled sharply and exhaled. "It's still partially there, along with wolf and bat."

Gunner grumbled, "It's how they evaded detection so long. When they're not shifted into their mutant side, you can't sniff them out."

It reminded her of Brock's claim that in the alley the pair he'd been tailing just disappeared. In reality, they'd simply shifted.

"Meaning if you see a human, aim to kill. Got it." She took the stairs quickly, expecting someone to ask them their business.

In the eerie stillness, a scream suddenly erupted. Then gunfire. She ran, taking the steps two at a time and arriving on a scene of pure chaos.

Blood dripped from the ceiling. Probably jetted from the corpse missing its head, which appeared to have been torn off and tossed at a hanging chandelier that still swung with its sightless prize.

More gunfire, this time closer, had her whirling to see a man aiming a gun at something stalking toward him. A creature drenched in blood, walking on two legs, but huge, hairy, and angry.

"Shit is that..." Gunner trailed off.

It was Brock, and they'd arrived too late judging by the way he roared and lunged for the guy with the gun. He ripped it from the soldier's hands and began beating him with it before snapping it over his knee. The guy tried to run. Brock leaped and landed in front of him. He cracked the man over his leg and dropped him to the ground.

He wasn't done, though. Another head went flying. There would be no healing from that.

"What do we do?" Gunner sounded pained.

"Nothing. That's Brock." She could see it in his tortured gaze as it suddenly fell on her.

He froze in place but trembled. She took a step in his direction then another.

Movement flipped her head to see a man and woman trying to sneak past.

"Don't let them escape," Gunner growled before lunging for them.

It drew Brock's attention, whereas she had her gaze tugged higher overhead to a balcony over the massive hall where they held most receptions.

Luis stood there gripping the rail.

The man who tried to kill her and her father. Who'd caused all kinds of trouble.

Brock followed Gunner through an arch into the east wing of the house after the doctor and his sister.

She chose to help him over vengeance. As she sprinted in his direction, her father snarled, "Luis is mine."

She chased the human pair past the sitting room with its metal blinds drawn closed. Snarling and thumping preceded her arrival into the library, a place she spent a lot of time in, mostly because the flock didn't. She'd once asked her father why he didn't turn more cerebral types. According to him, he did, but the blood lust changed them.

The doctor and his sister hid behind a wall of four creatures, the rabid version that had been released from the cages placed in the library. She might have wondered why they didn't attack the man who'd broken them until she noticed the doctor held up his phone and smirked.

"He's somehow signaling them to do his bidding," Gunner remarked as she came alongside. He'd gone left upon entering. Brock, on the other hand, advanced.

"We have to help him. Four is too many."

She inched left to flank just as the monsters attacked. Her worry about Brock proved misplaced. He swung his arms, connecting hard with one creature, sending it reeling. He whirled and tore into the next, using his jaw to clamp and worry flesh until he tore out a chunk.

The only reason she wetted her blade was because one armless monster came hissing in her direction. She dispatched it in time to see Brock advancing on the doctor.

"Stop. I command you." The doctor aimed his phone. "I gave you the chip in that second injection. You must obey."

Brock spat something at him. "I don't think so." He then grabbed the doctor, digging in his clawed fingers and tore him apart, literally ripping him in two.

A woman screamed, and Arianna glanced to see

the sister running for an exit, only to have Gunner block her path. She veered and came face to face with one of her brother's creations.

She pointed at Gunner and offered a shrill, "Kill him. I command you."

The monster snarled and lunged for Joella, slashing her across the face before slamming her to the floor. A single gunshot to the head fired by Gunner and the beast collapsed atop Joella's prone body.

Across the carnage, Arianna's gaze met Brock's, his face his and not. He'd maintained a mostly human aspect, if with wilder hair and sideburns. A sexy Wolverine character came to mind, down to the beautiful, tortured eyes.

He howled, a man in agony.

A mate in need.

She held out her hand to him and whispered his name.

And what did he do?

He ran away.

18

BROCK RETAINED enough wits to realize he'd lost control. It wasn't the blood on his skin or in his mouth that led to that conclusion, or the various bodies strewn in his wake, but seeing the shock in Arianna's eyes.

"Brock?" She reached for him.

He recoiled, terrified he'd hurt her. Fearing her disgust.

He ran. His nose and feet knew the way to freedom. He encountered the front door and flung it open onto a cloudy day, the air heavy with moisture. As he stepped outside, ready to flee, he heard her behind him.

"Where do you think you're going, puppy?" she huffed, trying to sound light, but he heard the anxiety in her tone.

"Get back inside!" he growled.

"Not unless you come with me." She sounded closer.

He glanced to the sky. If the sun came out... "Get in the house, princess." The words were guttural in this monster shape.

"Not without you." She touched his shoulder. "Look at me."

"No. I don't want you to see me like this."

"Isn't that my line?" she drawled, tugging at him.

"I'm a monster," was his hushed reply.

"Am I a monster because I drink blood?"

"No!" His reply was vehement as he whirled to face her.

"And neither are you." She cupped his cheek. "We do what we must to survive."

"Speaking of which, you should get in the house before the sun emerges." He glanced to the sky. Dark and heavy with clouds but also moving rapidly.

"Not unless you come with me."

Just as he was about to refuse, what he feared most happened. The clouds split, and a ray of sun beamed down to bathe her in its glow.

He didn't think; he panicked. He tucked her to his chest and ran for the shadows found just past the door frame. He kicked the portal shut and only then set her down to inspect her.

"I'm fine."

He didn't believe her. The sun burned Vampires. "I'm so sorry."

She slapped at his hands. "I'm serious, puppy. Don't ask me how, but the sun didn't burn me."

He finally looked at her. Her unblemished skin. The annoyed curve of her lips and glint in her eyes. "How is that possible?"

"I don't know, but I'll wager it has something to do with you."

"Me?"

She nodded. "My father said a mating bond between a Vampire and a Lycan could have special traits."

"He knows about us!" He retained enough wits to realize that probably wasn't a good thing.

"He does, and before you run off again, he's given his approval."

That rounded his mouth. "Well shit." Then he added, "So you know we're mated? Which I will add I didn't do on purpose. By the time I bit you, it had already happened."

She snorted. "I'm aware, and lucky for you, I'm good with it."

"Are you sure?"

She cupped his cheek. "I can't believe I'm saying this, but we're meant to be together."

"I love you, princess."

"My first and last, puppy," she replied with a wink.

He dragged her close for a hug, not ready to kiss, not with him still swollen and monstrous. She didn't seem to care as she gripped him tight and wiggled.

A moment of intimacy shattered when Gunner strutted past, complaining, "Get a room!"

Arianna turned around and flashed a finger. "Blow a statue, you cold bastard. We got him back."

"Did we?" Gunner eyed Brock up and down. "You okay, bro?"

"Not really, but at least I'm not hungry anymore." The adrenaline had finally worn off, along with the bloodlust of before. As if a balloon, he felt himself suddenly deflating, his body shrinking back to his usual self.

Thank fuck the whole monster thing wasn't permanent.

Gunner waited for his shift to finish before saying, "Looking better now. How do you feel?"

"Okay, I guess," Brock said with a grimace. "Thanks for coming to the rescue." He included Arianna in that statement, drawing her back to his side.

His friend arched a brow. "Didn't look like you needed much help."

A reminder that the blood all over came about as a result of him going a little wild. "The doctor is dead. I killed him." That he remembered. "I also eliminated a Cabal member called Dmitri."

Gunner nodded. "Good. Joella was taken out by the monsters in the library. Speaking of which, I took out a pair in the kitchen."

"I got only one because someone was hogging them." Arianna pouted, which was when Bernie limped in, bandanna askew, to cough, "Sorry I'm late. I had a creature to deal with in the basement."

As for Lord Augustus, he entered holding Luis' severed head, the eyes still wide open in surprise. Augustus beamed. "Well, that was a lot of excitement."

Arianna pointed. "Why are you walking around with his head? Toss it in the trash where it belongs."

"I have a better idea, Nina. Bernie, fetch me a hat box, would you? And some packing tape. I want to mail a package."

"To who?" Gunner blurted out.

"His family." Augustus dangled the prize, and his smile held cold vengeance when he said, "Apparently it's time I reminded another flock why coming after my family is a bad idea."

Old Brock might have thought it a tad bloodthirsty. A mated Brock agreed wholeheartedly because he never wanted to see Arianna threatened again. "Let me know if you need a hand."

"I will. Oh, and while I'm sure you already know

this, hurt my daughter and you will end up mounted on my wall." With that warning and a cheerful smile, Augustus wandered off with Bernie.

Gunner shook his head. "Fuck me, but I kind of like the guy." He then grimaced at Brock. "Dude, while your junk is impressive, find some pants."

"What he needs is a shower. Let's go," Arianna ordered.

"Go where?"

Rather than say, she dragged him to the second floor of the east wing to her bedroom suite. It included a sitting room, bedroom, and a bathroom bigger than his last apartment. She shoved him into the shower, the hot water immediately sluicing the grime from his skin, swirling pink as it went down the drain.

She soaped him head to foot while he tried to find his wits and failed. Fatigue pulled him enough that he didn't protest as she put him to bed.

Her bed. It helped she climbed in beside him and snuggled against his side, whispering, "Don't worry, rest. I'm here and not going anywhere."

It was all he needed to fall asleep.

And when he woke?

She woke with him, her hands finding his cock under the blanket and needing only a few strokes to have him ready.

She climbed atop him and rode, a princess, a

goddess, his lover, his mate. They came together in passion, their climax affirming their connection that didn't need words, but he said them anyway. "I love you."

Trust her to be a brat and say, "Well duh. Now show me how you worship a princess."

He did, using his tongue and fingers on her until she called him god.

And then he made her see heaven.

EPILOGUE

THE CLEANUP TOOK place while Brock and Arianna recovered—which involved them not leaving her bedroom for a full day. No one seemed to mind given they'd prevailed.

Sascha was dead. His research destroyed. As for his creations? Being hunted down to ensure they weren't a contagion that might spread.

Unfortunately, Joella wasn't found among the dead, which surprised but, given her injuries, and humanity, shouldn't pose a problem.

Luis' head had been mailed off, and Augustus eagerly awaited the reply. It would most likely end in a blood feud, even though there was no excuse for an heir of another flock to indulge in such a heinous act.

Dmitri's death was reported to the Cabal by Brock, who took the time to also explain how he'd not only betrayed the Lycans but also caused a schism with Lord Augustus and the Vampires. The Cabal offered apologies. It wasn't enough. Arianna made it clear Brock would be taking Dmitri's spot or else.

Brock might have argued more, except for the fact someone had to do the job and not be a corrupt fucker at the same time. Perhaps he could effectuate change from within.

In better news, the serum that the mad doctor injected didn't cause lasting damage. Brock's Lycan heritage treated it like a virus and eradicated it. As for his other new traits? The fact he could now flip into wolfman and not just wolf, was stronger, could smell better... According to Arianna and her father, he had their mating bond to blame for that. But he wasn't the only one to benefit. Arianna could step into the sun for minutes at a time before her skin tingled. They could also mind-speak up to a certain range, which could be startling when he dealt with people and she suddenly would be in his head saying things like, *I'm naked and need you.*

It might have taken ten years to get to this point, but they'd finally made it. She was all his, and as of this evening, they had moved out of the compound into the partially renovated carriage house.

Tradesmen had been working on it overtime, finishing off the space and furnishing it in the last few days. When Arianna dragged him there rather than to the dining room for dinner, he'd wondered at her haste.

The main floor of the carriage house had been turned into a garage replete with tools and a new wreck to work on. The top floor was a public area to entertain if they had people over. Their true home, though, was underground. Apart from a bedroom, bathroom, and kitchen, it included a living room area with a massive plush couch and, in front of it, a long table. It held a charcuterie board, cheese dip and chips, veggie sticks with a different dip, deep-fried bites of calamari, fish and shrimp, baguettes and more. The big screen television waited for their choice.

He glanced at her. "What's this?"

"I think it's past time we finally got our dinner and a movie, don't you think?"

He laughed. Something he had a feeling he'd be doing a lot more of.

As Arianna snuggled into him, he was more determined than ever to make sure nothing came between him and the woman he loved.

She pointed the remote and hit Play.

As the title credits ran, he groaned. "What kind of cruelty is this? You chose *Moulin Rouge* as our first date-night movie?"

She grinned as she popped a chicken nugget into her mouth. "What's wrong with it?"

"It's got singing," he grumbled.

"And dancing," she reminded.

He groaned. "So unfair. Why can't we do something like *Top Gun: Maverick* or *Dune*?"

"Because I actually want to see those movies."

He blinked. "I don't understand."

She took off her shirt and tossed it to the side, winked, and said, "I think you'll figure it out."

He did. Two times, and then managed a third when he presented her with a present, a violin, which she played after she strummed his instrument.

GUNNER EYED the flights leaving the UK. So many choices now that he had no village, no pack to call his own. He could have stayed in London. Lord Augustus himself offered him that choice given his service, even if unintentional, to the flock. But while Brock seemed comfortable among the Vampires, Gunner couldn't say the same.

He could have gone to Canada, where Quinn assured him Griffin, the Byward Pack alpha, would accept him with open arms. However, Gunner had spent enough time traveling around and not fitting in anywhere. Time to face the past. To make amends. To maybe find a way of moving forward.

Time to see if he still had a chance at happiness—and love. He boarded a flight to New York then took a connection to Georgia.

After more than a decade, he was going home.

WILL GUNNER GET A SECOND CHANCE WITH HIS ONE AND ONLY LOVE?

FIND OUT IN *WEREWOLF NOEL.*

For more books and fun see EveLanglais.com